A Very Private Life

Michael Frayn was born in London in
1933. He began his career as a reporter
and humorous columnist, first on the
Guardian and then on the *Observer*. He
has written five novels and a number of
plays, including *Alphabetical Order*,
Clouds, *Make and Break*, *Noises Off*, and
Benefactors. He has also translated for
the theatre, mostly from the Russian,
and published a philosophical work,
Constructions. He has continued to work
intermittently as a journalist, with
features for the *Observer* on Cuba, Israel,
Japan, and elsewhere, and with a series
of personal films for BBC Television on
Berlin, Vienna, Australia, Jerusalem,
and the London suburbs in which he
grew up.

The Russian Interpreter is also available
in Flamingo. *The Tin Men* and *Towards
the End of the Morning* will be published
in Flamingo during 1985 and *Sweet
Dreams* in 1986. Meanwhile, they are
available as Fontana paperbacks.

Michael Frayn

A Very Private Life

FLAMINGO

Published by Fontana Paperbacks

First published in Great Britain
by William Collins Sons & Co. Ltd 1968
First issued in Fontana Paperbacks 1981

This Flamingo edition first published
in 1984 by Fontana Paperbacks,
8 Grafton Street, London W1X 3LA

Reproduced, printed and
bound in Great Britain by
Hazell, Watson & Viney Limited,
member of the BPCC Group,
Aylesbury, Bucks.

Once upon a time . . .

Once upon a time there will be a little girl called Uncumber.

Uncumber will have a little brother called Sulpice, and they will live with their parents in a house in the middle of the woods. There will be no windows in the house, because there will be nothing to see outside except the forest. While inside there will be all kinds of interesting things – strange animals, processions, jewels, battles, mazes, convolutions of pure shapes and pure colours – which materialise in the air at will, solid and brilliant and almost touchable. For this will be in the good new days a long, long while ahead, and it will be like that in people's houses then. So the sight of the mud and grimy leaves outside would scarcely be of much interest.

Then again, windows might let the air in, and no one would want the congenial atmosphere of the house contaminated by the stale, untempered air of the forest, laden with dust and disease. From one year's end to the next they won't go outside, and the outside world won't come in. There will be no need; all their food and medicine and jewellery and toys will be on tap from the mains – everything they could possibly require will come to the house through the network of pipes and tubes and wires and electromagnetic beams which tangle the forest. Out along the wires and beams their

5

wishes will go. Back, by return, will come the
fulfilment of them.

A rich childhood

The fact that no one goes out and no one comes in
doesn't mean that they won't *see* anyone, of course.
They'll be seeing people all the time. Their relations,
their friends, the various official representatives of
society – they'll be materialising before them in the
special reception chambers, transmitted by way of the
wires and beams, and reproduced by the three-
dimensional holovision system in all their natural
solidity, at all hours of the day and night. Particularly
Aunt Symphorosa with the sad life and the perpetual
smile; and Great-great-grandfather, who will make
rather a habit of falling asleep while on transmission,
so that Uncumber's father won't know whether he can
politely switch him off or not. 'How can I watch the
Battle of Borodino on the history channel while your
blasted mother's grandfather is occupying the
reception chamber?' he complains to his wife – a family
joke.

If anything, in fact, they will see too much of their
friends and relations. There will be days when the
whole family remains in conclave for hours at a time –
Great-great-grandfather, Uncle Expeditus, Great-

great-great-aunt Pherbutha, Cousin Offa, Great Second Cousin Kenulf, the lot – none of them feeling that he is imposing upon the others, because he is still sitting quietly in his own home, and each of them feeling gravely imposed upon, because all the others are in his home, too. In fact, there will be scarcely any excuse left for not seeing everyone one ought to see, since seeing them will involve no more than selecting a number and pressing a switch.

Then there will be endless days when their parents' old friends Pelagius and Dympna materialise, together with their tiresome children. Their tiresome children are switched into Uncumber's and Sulpice's room, of course. Sulpice plays with them happily, because Sulpice is good and Sulpice likes everyone. But Uncumber gets spiteful, and reduces the visitors to tears by constantly switching them off. Uncumber will be a difficult child, there's no doubt about it.

And they'll see a lot of the world. They'll have memorable family holidays together – weeks on a lonely shore where the sun shines all day, on and on, and the surf booms, and the fine salt spray drifts over them in the wind, riming their brown skins with white. On these holidays they hear peasants singing in the fields when the wind drops in the evening. Far out to sea at midday squadrons of tall yachts cross the track of the sun and spread out with dreamy slowness. One holiday they see a schooner with a black hull creep in just before sunset, its rusty brown sails flapping in the evening calm, the pop-pop-pop of its engine clearly audible over the still water. It anchors in the roads, and when it sails again the following morning it's riding higher in the water; the children will believe they heard the splash of oars during the night, and the scrunch of a small boat on the sand . . .

It's always sad at the end of these holidays. Uncumber hates the moment when the hot sun and the spume blower are turned off, and the whole salt, open, white-and-blue world collapses into nothingness, leaving them alone in their rooms again, with the empty Imaginin packets, and holovision chambers vacant for the arrival of Great-great-great-aunt Pherbutha.

The facts of life

Uncumber can just remember the arrival of Sulpice.

It was when she was three. A large parcel arrived through the delivery tube for her mother, and her mother became strangely excited and shy about it.

'What is it? What is it?' shouted Uncumber. 'Is it for me? Is it my birthday?'

'No, it's somebody else's birthday,' said her mother, laughing in a strange way, and blushing, and kissing Uncumber as she tore the wrapping off the parcel.

There inside was a transparent container, full of liquid. And in the liquid, rolled up in a ball with its eyes tight shut, was a tiny baby!

'Oh! Oh! Oh!' cried her mother, laughing and crying. 'Isn't he beautiful? Look at his little feet! Oh,

Cumby!'

'Is he really for us?' asked Uncumber doubtfully.

'Yes, Cumby – he's your brother!'

'But how did they know we wanted one?'

'Because, don't you remember, Daddy and I sent off the things to make him with, and asked them to make us a little boy? Don't you remember, Cumby? Now, let's look at the instructions for unpacking him . . .'

What happens when you die

'Do you die when you get old, Mummy?' Uncumber will ask one day.

'Sometimes,' her mother replies.

'What happens to you when you die?'

'Oh, you take some special medicine, and you get better again.'

'But *I* mean, if you really, *really* die?'

'Well, if you really die very badly, then I suppose you're put in the tube, and you go on to another place.'

'Which tube? The waste tube?'

'I suppose so . . .'

'And you're chopped up into little pieces, like the old packaging?'

'I think so . . . But really, there's no need to worry about it, it won't happen for hundreds of years yet.'

'Hundreds and hundreds and hundreds and

hundreds?'

'Well, hundreds.'

Uncumber thinks about the great world outside the house, from which one arrives so neatly packaged, and to which one returns so finely ground.

'What's it like outside, Mummy?' she asks.

'Well, you know, dear,' says her mother, exasperated by the metaphysical unanswerability of this question. 'You see it in the holovision chambers all the time.'

'No, *I* mean, what's it *really* like?'

'That *is* what it's really like. Don't ask silly questions, dear.'

Animals

One of the earliest of Uncumber's remarks to pass into the family folk-lore will be about the repairmen. Whenever something goes wrong with the house – when the protein supply gets blocked, say, or the holovision chambers go on the blink – the repairmen come down from the sky and strip panels off the outer walls until they find the fault.

One day she will hear the familiar clink of their tools on the other side of the wall, and their muffled talk and laughter, and she will say: 'The animals are there again!'

It's all mixed up inside her head with some holovision programme she has seen. She thinks people live inside, and animals outside.

And she takes everything so seriously. One day her mother will find her *tapping back* to the repairmen! And the repairmen answering her taps! She will be only five at the time, so her mother will be more amused than alarmed. Who but Uncumber would have managed to get in communication with the outside classes at the age of five! But when her mother gently dissuades her, Uncumber is furious. She weeps and throws herself on the floor and shouts that she wants to see the 'animals'.

'Oh, come on, Cumby! You see plenty of animals.'

'No, I mean *see* them! Really *see* them!'

'Anyway, they're not animals. They're people, just like you and me.'

'Why are they outside, then? Why aren't they inside?'

'Some people are on the inside – some are on the outside. That's just the way the world is, Cumby.'

Tapping at the animals – this becomes another of the family's jokes, of course. But at the time Uncumber gets almost hysterical about it. She has to be quietened down with a quick shot of calmant. She will need many more such shots throughout her childhood.

Sulpice will be quite different. He will be amenable and easy-going from the first; a delightful child, who never gives his parents a moment's anxiety.

Incidentally, their father's name will be Aelfric, their mother's Frideswide. These names will seem ridiculous and embarrassing to Uncumber when she gets old enough to mind about such things. No doubt they *will* be rather old-fashioned by then. Why, she will wonder miserably, couldn't they have been called something sensible? Frumentius and Osyth, for instance, like her friend Rhipsime's parents.

Of course, if they had been called Frumentius and Osyth she would no doubt have found something funny about these names too. This is the way children always repay the thoughtfulness of those who ordered them – particularly Uncumber! She *will* be a difficult child!

Out

Uncumber and Sulpice have this game they play, of *trying to get out*. It is one of their legends that somewhere a secret door exists into the outside world. They whisper about it together in corners, and draw up plans, and press and peer and pry among the soft, yielding surfaces of the walls and ceilings. For Sulpice it is a purely metaphysical quest; he is not an imaginative child, and the idea that the search might actually have an outcome never occurs to him. If it did, he would never dream of taking part.

But one day – when they are not even looking seriously – they find the secret panel! Uncumber must have pressed a switch – or moved some kind of lever – she's no idea what it was she did. Because when she leans against the wall a section of the upholstery sinks inwards beneath her weight – a kind of door, which opens creaking upon a world of blackness.

They draw back, terrified, gazing into the hole from a safe distance. So that's how it is outside – black!

'We must tell Mummy!' says Sulpice.

But Uncumber won't let him. She creeps nearer, Sulpice dragging on her arm, and peers harder into the darkness, holding her breath.

'I can see some stairs,' she says. 'There are stairs going up. And there's a wall. It's a sort of room.'

'Come back! Come back!' cries little Sulpice.

But Uncumber doesn't answer. She is not at all surprised to discover that the outside world is enclosed by walls, just like the inside one. She puts her head into the door-way, and after she has acclimatised her head for a time, she puts a foot in. Then some tiny noise in the darkness brings all her simmering panic to the boil at once. She scrambles wildly back out of the hole, and presses on the projecting end of the panel until the door closes.

But they don't forget it. The secret door comes to dominate their lives. Each day they go back to it and open it, to renew their terror. Each day Sulpice pleads with Uncumber not to go in. But each day she does – and each day she goes a little farther. On to the first step of the stairs! On to the second!

'No, Cumby! Come back! Please, Cumby! Don't, Cumby!'

On to the third, and the fourth!

'*No*, Cumby! *Please* come back, Cumby!'

On so high into the darkness that Sulpice, straining to keep his feet in the inside world while his terrified eyes follow her, can see nothing but a white shape . . .

She gets to know the little outside world of the secret stairs by touch. The main differences between outside and inside, she works out, are that outside is dark and rather cold, with unnaturally and excitingly hard surfaces instead of upholstery, and that when she comes back the soles of her feet and the fingers of her exploring hands are grey.

'What is it?' cries Sulpice in alarm, the first time she shows him the grey discoloration.

'It's dust,' she explains. 'It's something they have outside – I've seen about it on the holovision.'

At the top of the secret stairs the outside world broadens out a little, she discovers, into a slightly more capacious darkness. She explores every inch with her hands, murmuring reassurances all the time to Sulpice, whose frightened questions filter up from below with the last ghost of the reflected light: 'Are you all right, Cumby? Are you still there, Cumby?' The outside world, she discovers, is bounded on all sides by walls, floor, and ceiling.

She is strangely disappointed at the smallness of it. The complete lack of animals troubles her, too.

And outer still

And then, one day when she is up in the little outside world at the top of the secret stairs, her elbow bangs against something sticking out. She pulls at it, and a great section of wall comes swinging back, filling the darkness with light. A whole new world opens in front of her, unbounded, unrecognisably confused – the *real* outside, as she grasps at once.

It all happens so suddenly, and what she sees is so strangely expected and yet unexpected, that she cannot afterwards remember at all clearly what it was. The first thing she notices, while she is still blinking in the sudden light, is the air. It moves! Erratically but tangibly it comes swirling in around her, whipping her hair into her eyes, rubbing over her skin with a strange coldness, so that she wraps her arms round herself to keep it out. And with the air comes the feel of dampness, and a smell – a wet, rank, vegetable smell.

The light, as soon as her eyes have adjusted to it, is diffuse and grey – not at all the sort of light that the holovision shows in the outside world. And the colours are all dim and muted. If she expected anything, from watching the holovision, it was a brilliant clear bowl of sky – green-blue tumbling seas – yellow sands. But the sky is a dusty grey, brightening in places to lemon yellow. There is no sea or sand, only a muddle of trees and undergrowth in greys and browns and mouldering dark greens.

She steps through the door. She is standing on the flat roof of the house, and all around, in every direction, is the choked dark tangle of the forest. She makes out straight lines and rational curves among it – grey pipes and wires running in every direction, intersecting at the grey pylons rising from overgrown clearings, and dipping down everywhere to other blind houses like her own. In some places the weeds and brambles are growing out of a crazed pattern of cracks in some hard grey substance – one of the old roads, perhaps, which used to cover the inhabited world like a net, now abandoned and returning to the disorder they were stamped upon.

The first object with any notable colour in it that Uncumber sees is one which she doesn't at first recognise – a dull, orange-red disc hanging without visible means of support in the yellower part of the sky. Black flakes flutter down and settle on her shivering shoulders.

And then the wind swirls harder, and the door slams shut behind her.

Blue skin

Uncumber beats her palms against the door, and screams. She shivers with cold and blind terror. To be shut out alone in this huge unpeopled muddled grey nothingness! She presses herself against the door, as if trying to melt back into it.

She is not alone for long. There is a loud, complaining whine from the sky overhead, and another house comes swooping down. She watches it over her shoulder, hypnotised into silence. It stops a few feet above the roof, a door opens in the bottom, and two men jump out.

At first she scarcely recognises them as men. They've no skin! Or no normal skin. From neck to toe they're covered in a strange dark blue stuff! Is it dark blue skin? Or is it something they have wrapped round outside their skins? She begins to scream all over again.

'What's the matter, love?' asks one of them.

'Locked out, are you?' says the other.

'Come on, now, be a good girl.'

Their voices sound human enough, even rather reassuring. All the more frightening, that these strange blue skins should have reassuring human voices.

She closes her eyes, fills her head with scream, and makes a wild, inhuman effort to press her body through the solid door.

You never know who you may meet

In which effort she succeeds.

She tumbles headlong back into the house, as the door is flung open by her father. He has come running white-faced up the secret stairs to look for her, warned by Sulpice. There are confused explanations between her father and the men in the blue skins, then father and daughter are stumbling back down the stairs, and mother is giving everyone, including herself, shots of calmant to restore some sense of order and sanity to the house.

When at last they are all entirely calm, and Uncumber's sobs have died away, Aelfric asks her gently to promise that she will never ever go outside again. She nods, still too shocked to speak.

'For a start,' he explains, 'you might get ill, Cumby. If you've lived all your life in air that's specially clean, and just the right temperature, you can't expect to resist the heat and cold of the air outside, and all the dirt and infection it carries. Those Kind People who found you – they were wearing *clothes*, weren't they, and special masks over their faces. You can't go outside without wrapping your body up to protect it.

'And secondly, you never know who you may meet out there. You see, Cumby, not everyone in the world is the same. There are different sorts of jobs which have to be done, and different sorts of people to do them. Some of us have to spend our lives inside, doing all the world's thinking and arguing and persuading. Somebody has to persuade other people that their little girls need more dolls to play with, for example. Somebody has to decide what we're going to do about the world's air shortage. And so on.

'Of course, people who do this sort of job have to sit at home, just like I do, so that they can see what's going on in the world at the touch of a switch, and talk to all the people thay have to talk to, and be in touch with all their various thinking and doing machines.

'But then there are other people who have to work outside. If your new doll gets jammed in the delivery tube on its way here, someone has to go out and unjam it! Someone has to put the delivery tube up in the first place! Well, this is the job of your great friends the "animals". Only, of course, not all animals are clever enough even to do this sort of work. Nowadays the four-legged animals don't usually do any work at all. It's just the two-legged ones, who can talk and think like us.'

Uncumber thinks about all this.

'Where do they live?' she asks. 'In the trees?'

Her father laughs.

'No, no,' he assures her. 'They have perfectly good homes.'

'Like ours?'

'Well, a bit different, because as I say they're rather different sort of people.'

'Were those two men in the blue skins animals?'

'Sort of. They were Kind People, who go round in their flying houses helping people in trouble, and keeping an eye on things. Because, you see, not all the animals in the forest are nice. Most of them are. But some of them try to get inside the houses, to hurt the people and take all the things away.'

'Why?'

'Because they're unhappy. But you see why we were so worried when you went outside? Inside this house you're part of a secure and happy world which stretches all over the globe. Step outside it, and you're in another world altogether – the old primeval world, Cumby, where anything can happen.'

Aelfric knows what he's talking about, too. He's a decider. All day he sits watching the holovision manifestations coming in from all over the earth, as often as not of events in the outside world, deciding disputes between people and 'animals', or between 'animal' and 'animal'.

If other people knew what he knows, they wouldn't go round the way they do shouting about the 'animals' being really just as happy as anybody else. In his private opinion, *everyone* in the outside classes is unhappy, or else ready to start being unhappy as soon as your back's turned. If he had his way, he'd put the lot of them on compulsory medication.

Dark glasses

They live a bit like animals themselves, Uncumber and
Sulpice, while they are still young – playing together,
running about the house, taking tumbles, and being
picked up to be kissed and comforted by their parents.
Children need this physical, tactile experience, of
course.

But as they grow older their lives become less
physical, and more private. Another room will be
added, for Uncumber to move out into, and the more
she and Sulpice become involved in absorbing
educational holovision, the less chance either of them
have to move out of their rooms. Their parents will
gradually find it more convenient to manifest
themselves to their children at the touch of a switch,
rather than drag themselves wearily to their feet and
come looking for them in the flesh. And as the brilliant
physical energy of early childhood subsides, and the
lethargy of adolescence approaches, the children find it
easier to do the same, even with each other. From one
day's end to the next they scarcely move out of their
rooms – hardly even shift off the gentle cushion of air
which keeps them comfortably suspended an inch or
two above their couches, except to exercise their
muscles on their private exercising machines.

And they enter upon another, more intimate privacy.
They are no longer allowed to go naked, but are

expected to wear their dark glasses all the time, like adults. Uncumber will have tantrums about this, of course.

'Why do I have to wear them?' she will pout, sprawling back on her air-layer rebelliously.

'Because it's not decent to go around with bare eyes at your age,' her mother explains. 'You don't see me or your father going around with bare eyes.'

'But *why* not?'

'Because it's not decent – that's why not! You want to keep *some* things to yourself, don't you? You don't want everyone seeing exactly how you feel and exactly what you're thinking all the time. It might put ideas into their heads.'

'What sort of ideas?'

'Well . . . it might encourage them to be over-familiar. It would let them know what you're thinking and feeling. They could see whether you like them or not.'

So they wear dark glasses about the house. But even at the age of fourteen and fifteen Uncumber will often forget hers, or wear them pushed casually up on her forehead, so that her eyes are exposed. This infuriates her father – and the first big rows of her increasingly stormy adolescence are over the dark glasses.

'Slolloping about the house stark naked – it's disgusting!' shouts her father.

'Half-naked,' corrects Uncumber. 'They're on my forehead.'

'Put them on properly at once.'

'I don't see why I should wear stupid blinkers over my eyes just to please you!'

'You'll do what you're told!'

'I won't!'

'Don't talk to me like that, my girl!'

'Why don't you take a shot of calmant if you don't like it? Then you won't mind about it any more.'

'My God! You're the one who should be taking the shots! You're the one who's causing the disturbance!'

And snap – snap! They slam their switches down to shut each other off.

She won't take her medicine

And this issue of the shots is another of the themes of her adolescence. She won't take her Pax, or her Distractin, or any of the other calmants and hallucinogens which are necessary for laying the foundations of good health and building a sound character. It's not really the principle she objects to. It's just the phase she's going through of rebelling against parental authority. Everyone has to go through it, of course, but it's particularly violent in her case – because she won't take the necessary medicaments to control it. It's a vicious circle. And the further it goes, the more likely it becomes that she will be stuck with the forms of her rebellion. Long after the rebellion has finished she'll go on refusing to take her medicaments, and looking for outside reasons to justify her obstinacy.

It's scarcely necessary to say that Sulpice will take *his* shots. He soon learns the skill of maintaining himself in emotional equilibrium, and of preparing himself for the various sessions of instructions, imagery, and individual psychic guidance which are available on the holovision, and by which the human mind and character are developed.

He is immensely gifted intellectually. Naturally – he treats himself with Intel and Concentrin and the rest. Over and over again he tries to catch Uncumber's interest in the world which this opens up.

'What I'm working on at the moment,' he tells her, 'is hyperequality. Not the same as superidentity, of course! In fact one might say the two terms are starkly infraparallel! We use hyperequality to define the notion of zero-negative, which in turn gives us a zero-position defined by the series $k_1S(x-l)$, $k_2S(x^2-l)$, $k_3S(x^3-l)$ etc., where k remains marginally plasmatic...'

But of course she can't follow even these elementary moves. She still feels close to him – even in these moods of high intellectual dilation. She admires his ease and grace, his natural acceptance of life. But not even he can persuade her out of her rebelliousness.

'Come on, Cumby!' he urges. 'Take your shot. It'll make you feel right inside – I promise you.'

'I don't want to feel *right*!' she argues. 'I want to feel *me*!'

'But Cumby, I feel *more* me after I've taken my shots. Honestly.'

'Look, I don't want to feel *more* anything! I just want to feel the same!'

'But, you don't feel *right* inside now! You don't, do you? Admit it.'

Uncumber buries her face in the fountaining air.

'Oh,' she moans, 'why can't everyone leave me alone?'

'Oh, Cumby!' sighs Sulpice.

She's a difficult child, there'll be no doubt about it. Her refusal to take her calmants will undoubtedly send up consumption by the rest of the family. Ridiculous that three people should have to keep dosing themselves just because the fourth one won't. Even Great-great-grandfather will be driven out of their reception chambers by her behaviour.

'Where have we gone wrong?' her parents will meditate, as they sit late at night full of Meditatin, watching the meditation channels.

She sulks while everyone is merry

And here's another way she upsets her parents – she won't laugh when she's supposed to. As the children get older they are expected to take part in their parents' social occasions. When Pelagius and Dympna call, for example, Uncumber and Sulpice are no longer supposed to share a separate reception chamber with their children. They are expected to lie switched in with the adults, taking a little Socion and a little Hilarin, and

25

laughing at the sort of things you laugh at after you've taken Socion and Hilarin.

For instance, everyone laughs helplessly when Aelfric balances a Hilarin pill on the end of his nose and tries to jerk it into his mouth. Aelfric is always very amusing on these occasions. He knows a lot of tricks with pills that make everyone relax and laugh and get into the spirit of the occasion. And he has a lot of very celebrated jokes which never fail to entertain, such as getting up from his air-couch, walking slowly and gravely round the holovision chamber in the middle of the room, and announcing: 'I'm a man who likes to see a thing from all sides!' Or the one where he pulls a frightful face and says: 'I'm just a plain man!' Everyone always laughs till he cries at these, of course, and by the time they see Aelfric getting ready to do the one where he puts his head under one of the food taps and says 'Food for thought,' they're usually begging for mercy, and gasping 'No, stop, stop!'

Everyone except Uncumber. She won't take her Socion and she won't take her Hilarin, so – unbelievable as it seems to everyone else – she manages to sit through these performances with a straight face. Not even a straight face, in fact – she scowls. She finds something horrible about these occasions. Even when Pelagius says, as he usually does, 'That reminds me of something, but I can't remember what!' she doesn't melt.

At one of these parties they all turn on her. 'Look at Cumby!' gasps her father, pointing at her. 'Have you ever seen such a look?' They all gaze at her in silence for a moment, their faces remote and speculative, walled off in their hilarity. Then gradually they start to laugh at her, until they all become more helpless than ever. Dympna falls off her couch on to the floor, and lies there, her shoulder-blades shaking spasmodically.

'You pigs!' shouts Uncumber. 'You disgusting pigs!'

And that's funnier than ever. The dark glasses slip down Frideswide's nose, and reveal her wet, closed eyes. Even Uncumber, with her famous libertarian attitude on dark glasses, is shocked by the sight. Someone will surely get rather seriously killed in this orgy, she thinks. The spasm will paralyse them – they will be unable to draw breath. She becomes frightened.

'Stop! Stop!' she cries. They shake their heads, waving feeble fingers at her in lieu of speech.

Uncumber is saved on this occasion because a grave-faced stranger suddenly manifests himself on the screen with a message for Aelfric, and everyone starts to laugh at this messenger instead. He wants Aelfric to make some urgent decisions on the situation which has emerged down in 471-533-902, where several thousand outside workers have rioted and fought a pitched battle with Kind People. Everyone sobs with laughter at this news. The man says there are at least 53 seriously dead – including 20 permanently so. 'Don't!' begs everyone. 'It's too funny! We can't bear it!'

Finally, his hands shaking with laughter, Aelfric takes down a syringe and injects himself with an emergency dose of Dehilarin and Judicor. The shaking stops almost immediately. He heaves a long deep sigh. The merry creases round his mouth disappear, and a certain melancholy spreads across the visible parts of his face.

'Just a moment,' he tells the messenger flatly. 'I'll switch these other people out of my chamber.'

After he has adjudicated the 471-533-902 dispute, he takes another dose of Hilarin and rejoins the party. Freshly charged, he makes such a noise that Uncumber can hear him through the wall, even though she has switched her own chamber off. There is no sound from the others; they must be too weary to laugh another syllable.

Later, after the party is over, Sulpice looks in to say a last yawning good night to her – and finds her laughing helplessly all by herself!

'What's the trouble, Cumby?' he asks anxiously.

'Oh, Sulpy!' she gasps. 'I felt so depressed that I took . . . I took . . . I took . . . I took . . . '

But she can't get the words out for laughing.

'You took some Hilarin?' asks Sulpice, astonished. 'You didn't, Cumby!'

She nods silently.

'But why *now*? After everyone's gone home?'

There is no sound from Uncumber except a faint, high, intermittent squeaking.

'Oh, Cumby!' sighs Sulpice.

How it was in days gone by

Sometimes her father will try to reason with her.

'Look, you don't know how lucky you are! If you'd been born in days gone by instead of now your life would be very different, I can tell you!

'In those days *everyone* had to go outside – even the inside classes! People lived in one place, and worked in another. And to get from the house where they lived to the house where they worked they had to go out in the air – thousands of them, millions of them, all brushing against each other and breathing in each other's faces! And they packed together in communal travelling houses – shoulder to shoulder, chest to chest!

'They did almost everything communally. They ate in crowds, worked in crowds, relaxed in crowds. Almost everywhere you went, you found yourself in the actual physical presence of other human beings. That's the literal truth, Cumby. I'm not telling you stories.

'Well, of course, they were rained on. And burnt by the sun – which was very strong in those days. And they were struck by lightning. And, of course, the contaminated air outside carried diseases; in those days people used to breathe in disease with every breath. And then naturally they'd pass the disease on to everyone around them, by touching them, or breathing over them. Everyone was diseased then, for at least a part of every year – diseased in the nose, so they

29

couldn't breathe properly; diseased in the throat, so they couldn't swallow; diseased in the stomach, so they couldn't digest; diseased in the head, so they couldn't think.

'And they were minced up by their travelling houses – crushed to death by the dozen inside them, ground up beneath them. You have to learn these things, Cumby. That's what it was like then. Even small children had to go outside, and breathe the unfiltered air, and mix with people they didn't like.

'They lived like animals – they behaved like animals. There was anarchy! But the reaction to anarchy was even worse. The most stringent order had to be imposed upon people, just so that they could survive their proximity. Society had to be arranged in strict hierarchical patterns, with powerful controls and sanctions. So that when people looked into the future all they could foresee was the necessity for stricter and stricter social order imposed by ever more powerful central authorities, through ever more far-reaching controls. One day, they feared, every aspect of human behaviour would be controlled by some central authority. Nothing would be private – not even people's thoughts. The whole of life would become public and communal. Freedom would vanish entirely.

'Well, of course, what in fact happened was exactly the opposite. *Everything* became private. People recognised the corruption of indiscriminate human contact, and one by one they withdrew from it. Whoever could afford it built a wall around himself and his family to keep out society and its demands. Gradually, as people's technological skills improved, the walls they built became more and more impenetrable. One by one the chinks which they were forced to leave in the fortifications in order to export their skills and import the necessities of life were closed up. All over the world each family with the intelligence and energy to manage it gradually created its own individual controlled environment. Each family built its own castle, into which nothing, whether food, air, information or emotion, was admitted until it had been purified and sterilised to suit the occupiers' needs.

'So we built the outer walls of our castles. And inside them we built inner walls to protect each member of the family from the proximity of the others.

'But, as we discovered, there were certain unwelcome intruders which seeped through all these defences. Uncertainty, discontent, anger, melancholy – neither filters nor electronic devices could keep them out. So we learnt to construct certain chemical screens inside our own bodies, and to retire behind them to an inner keep where *everything* was under our control.

'And in that inner keep, Cumby, we enjoy the perfect freedom which men have always dreamt of. What crippled and cut short all man's earlier experiments in freedom is that they were public; and the public freedom of one man must necessarily impinge upon the public freedom of others; so that public freedoms inevitably limit and destroy each other. But our modern *private* freedoms impinge upon no one and nothing. And no one and nothing can impinge upon them. Even death, the last and most inexorable invader of our privacy, is being driven back step by step.

'And that, Cumby, is why you've got to do what

you're told, and wear your dark glasses and take your pills – so that you can preserve the precious liberty that mankind has so slowly and so laboriously evolved.'

Uncumber will listen to all this in silence – scowling, no doubt, but attentive. One small point, however, will worry her.

'What about the outside people?' she will object. 'How are they perfectly free, if they're outside this controlled environment?'

Aelfric will sigh with exasperation.

'For heaven's sake, Cumby! They're not the same as us at all. They're entirely different.'

Waste

Uncumber thinks a good deal about those frightening times past when the sky was not grey but blue, and when the sun was too bright to have any colour at all – when it fired dry grass, parched whole tracts of the earth, and burned holes in the retinas of anyone who looked at it. Terrible times, when the world's population staggered thirst-wracked through the desert lands, clutching their sun-blinded eyes!

The sun looked then, in fact, as it looks now from the orbiting satellite cities above the earth. But the scattered waste-products of those cities have now, mercifully, dimmed the glare for those below. The sun's light is filtered through a blanket of combustion products mixed with atomised excrement, abandoned packaging materials, broken parts, and the unrecovered corpses of people killed in the various major satellite disasters. From this detritosphere a gradual slow precipitation occurs, as the particles sink into a descending orbit. The heavier items accelerate and burn up. The smaller particles fall slowly as a fine dust over the whole surface of the globe.

The topside of the detritosphere is beautiful, as everyone knows from watching the manifestations of it on their holovision. For hours at a time on the eidetic channels they show the changing patterns which the sun makes on it – foaming billows, purple in their shadowy depths, red and gold at their iridescent crests – individual pieces of dirty bath water breaking into irregular fragments full of silver light – full of golden light – full of the entire visible spectrum. It's the aesthetic experience which everyone can enjoy, as the countryside once used to be. They watch it with a shot of the appropriate hallucinogen inside them, and marvel over it, and secretly try to compose poems about it.

Uncumber's unmedicated melancholy makes her scornful of such commonplace prettinesses. She prefers to let her mind run upon the grey underside of the detritosphere, and the great waste-grounds on the earth below, where the various radioactive waste-products are taken to be dumped, and buried under insulating strata of mining spoil, ash, slag, and sewage-barren deserts, stretching rawly grey for hundreds of miles. She yearns to visit them, and to mope wanly about

33

them. She feels that it would be sweet to be contaminated with their radioactivity, and to decay with them in the pale yellow light.

The romanticism of her adolescence, in fact, is the romanticism of waste and decay. She is almost physically conscious of the energy being sucked out of the energy-bearing materials of the universe, and of the gradual conversion of the whole structure to exhausted sludge. She feels the process working in her – feels that her life is essentially tragic.

She thinks of those family holidays beneath a blazing sun and a brilliant blue sky. How humiliating to think that she once believed in them – believed they were manifestations of some actual beach, beneath an actual sun and an actual sky! Only a child would be taken in by such obvious fictions, of course. But what about all the other manifestations of the outside world which even adults accept as true? How can you believe in anything you see? For all anyone knows it is all simulated somewhere, just like the holiday scenes.

She laughs bitterly at her family, to think of them being taken in by this world of appearances; bursts into tears easily; seems more secretive and remote than ever. She needs a friend to confide in. But her old friend Rhipsime wouldn't understand thoughts like these at all. And how do you find a friend when you never meet anyone?

She should advertise for someone

And this will be a difficulty. The communications system of the inside world will be highly selective. One will on the whole see only people one intends to see, and since one can scarcely intend to see people of whose existence one is unaware, one will in effect see only people one knows already.

Of course, there are exceptions. New faces will manifest themselves in one's reception chamber from time to time – samplers collecting direct sample votes on proposed legislation, supply directors soliciting instructions for future deliveries of goods. Uncumber's friend Rhipsime claims she has seduced three of these callers. There's nothing more natural, she says; they expect it – think of it as part of the job. Uncumber is appalled by the idea. To her all these official visitors seem far too finished, too word-perfect, too faultlessly armoured, as they smile impersonally from behind their stylish dark glasses. She can no more understand Rhipsime than Rhipsime can understand her.

Uncumber pins greater hopes on meeting someone who turns up in her chamber on a wrong number. There are quite a lot of wrong numbers, of course, since every inside person in the world has a holovision chamber, and they can all dial each other. The faces of unknown old men, young girls, and children appear briefly, then disappear as soon as they have discovered their mistake. Uncumber can picture the sort of face she yearns to tell everything to – a man's face, young, but not too young; sympathetic; strong; idealistic. Few faces approaching this specification turn up on wrong numbers; and whenever one with even the remotest suggestion of suitability does, she somehow becomes confused, and snaps at it, all red and gruff.

She goes through a wild phase of misdialling deliberately herself. But the results are painfully similar.

There is a way, of course, for getting round the rigid selectivity of social life – otherwise new relationships would never be formed; she should advertise on one of the human market channels. She watches these advertisements for hours at a time. There are people of all ages offering themselves for every conceivable sort of relationship. Here's a girl looking for a timid boy to dominate. Here's an older man who has just lost his father looking for a substitute to whom he can continue to express his guilt. A woman wants a wild, ungrateful boy to mother. A young woman wants a man to set up house with and have children by. A man wants a friend who will let himself be betrayed and cheated, and still come back for more.

A serious-looking young man appears, raises himself from his air-couch to a polite reclining position, turns his head this way and that way, smiles, looks wistful, and smiles again, while the voice on the sound track says: 'Jarlath had genuinely normal relations with his parents in childhood, and has matured through three rich physical relationships, one of them of a rather interestingly homosexual nature. He is now seventeen, and feels ready for a brief but fairly intense relationship with a woman who can produce evidence of at least ten years' thorough experience in this field. He has no problems he needs sympathy with.'

But Uncumber cannot imagine applying for Jarlath, or for any of the others like him. Nor can she seriously imagine advertising herself. What would she say? – 'Bad-tempered, rebellious girl with no experience of any sort of relationship at all except arguing with her parents, and with her head full of romantic ideas about death and decay, seeks . . .' What? '. . . to sink herself without trace in someone; what sort of someone she finds difficult to say, but she is sure she will recognise him when she sees him . . .'

How she consoles herself

Of course, she is not unhappy all the time. She is capable of losing herself in the manifestations on the bespoke daydream channel, just like everyone else. For all her high-minded melancholy, she finds the spectacle of herself and her romantic adventures deeply consoling. For it's not just herself, but herself as she feels she trembles on the verge of being – beautiful, calm, radiant with individual identity, charged with some mystic sense of quest. And this fully realised self runs lightly through the cool green forest, finding grievously injured young men whose wounds she tends, and who, on recovery, turn out to be princes injured in the chase, with crystal palaces on mountain-tops to which they bear her off . . .

'Such nonsense!' she tells herself scornfully from time to time, but goes on watching, feeling secretly: 'In a way, after all, this *is* the real truth about me. This is how I am underneath . . .'

A trip to the mountains

Sulpice has found someone, of course, being Sulpice. He advertised, and had 74 replies, out of whom, after thorough interviewing, he picked a calm, lethargic girl called Nanto-Suleta.

Their relationship is perfect. They turn on their holovision and lie for hours beside each other's manifestation – perfectly still, but going through great ranges of sexual experience prepared for by careful medication with Libidin, and triggered by Orgasmin.

Sulpice tells Uncumber about these experiences sometimes.

'If you've never been through it yourself, you really can't begin to imagine it,' he says grandly, as she lies pretending not to listen, racked with curiosity and jealousy. 'You move through whole landscapes, legendary landscapes, full of rich greens and browns, with purple distances. You seem to be going southwards, because all the time the light becomes warmer and more golden. The earth teems with profusion – vineyards and cornfields, and orange groves with standing water about the roots of the trees, catching the sun. There are a great many people moving on the roads – strong, sinewy men with weathered skins driving donkeys and pack-horses, and singing as they go. Beyond the fields you catch glimpses of walled cities – honey-coloured stone, with towers and domes beyond. Everywhere you look there are little cities tucked away among the landscape! Armed men stand upon their gates; angels with long blue dresses and trumpets alight upon their battlements. In the still, quiet air you can hear voices within their walls – street cries, snatches of song, laughter.

'For several weeks the great company of pilgrims – as it now seems – presses on through this rich valley with ever lighter steps. Where are we going? We all know – though we couldn't say it.

'And then, quite suddenly, we are among the hills. Blue, rolling hills seem to lift from among the corn and fruit all around us. Effortlessly we glide among them. The landscape grows wilder. Not vineyards now but wild grapes – not corn but aromatic bushes, filling the air with warm southern smells. The whole company strip prickly pears off the roadside cactuses, and gorge themselves on the soft yellow fruit.

'We spend a month or more in these sweet uplands.

'And at the end of that time we realise with astonishment that we have wandered on to higher and higher ground, where the light has become dazzlingly clear, and the air is so thin that our hearts race at the slightest exertion, and our breath comes quickly. The whole teeming world of green-brown-gold and c+itied plains is stretched out behind and beneath us. In front of us, enormous ramparts of rose-coloured rock soar into the sky. We tilt our heads back to gaze at them, and slowly, slowly we grow light on our feet – our feet leave the ground! Still singing our pilgrim hymns in thin, bell-like counterpoint, we drift gently upwards, our immense eagle wings spread to catch some imperceptible updraught! The great rock towers come slowly nearer and nearer. The air is so thin and sharp that our voices tremble and shatter. Our eyes are fixed on the crest of the rock, because we know that as soon as we draw level with it we shall come face to face with the rising sun!

'And, Cumby, *forty-seven days* we float upwards like that! Sometimes the draught seems to halt, and hold us immobile over the emptiness beneath. We drift down a little, even! And then, upwards again! All around you can hear the faint cries and sighs of the pilgrims – though I think every sound must come from oneself, because there's no sign of anyone else around at this great height.

'I can't tell you much about those extraordinary days when you at last rise above the ridge from the west, and come face to face with the sun rising from the east. Except to say that the sun is much, much closer than you could ever have thought, and that you dissolve into its warmth and light with the utmost ease.

'And remain there, suspended in solution . . .

'Then you're rushing down from the mountain-top

into the valley beyond – running down the sheer rock-faces, trailing golden light from your hair and outstretched arms. Down and down you race – and it takes several days, you've got so far to go! – into a deep valley filled with the utmost silence. Pine trees line the floor and walls of the valley, absorbing every slightest sound, and among them – a lake, still and impenetrably dark. Then up you go again, soaring through the pines on the far side of the valley, your feet scarcely touching the ground, up on to the next mountain ridge. A period of serene, sunlit contemplation here, and then on down, like the wind, into the valley beyond.

'So up and down you soar, from valley to mountain, from mountain to valley, sometimes planing like the eagle, sometimes bounding like the chamois, sometimes galloping like a herd of mountain ponies. Until at last the mountains subside into hills again, and you drift down from the last of them into the warm, sunlit sea, and float there, calm and still, eyes closed, until evening.'

Sulpice lies back on his air-cushion and gazes at the ceiling. Uncumber looks at him irritably.

'You got all those ideas out of books and off the holiday manifestations,' she complains. 'How could you possibly know what mountains are really like?'

'That doesn't make the experience any the less valid,' says Sulpice calmly.

'It's all just inside your head.'

'Of course! That's where the world is centred, Cumby, inside your head!'

Uncumber thinks about it for some time, plucking at her lip with nervous crossness.

'Do you both take your dark glasses off?' she asks suddenly.

Sulpice blushes.

'Sometimes,' he says.

A picture of the mountaineers

This is how one of these excursions to the mountains appears to Uncumber, when Sulpice and Nanto-Suleta accidentally leave their circuit open one day:

Sulpice: Goldenly!

Nanto-Suleta: Yes!

Sulpice: A snakish goldenliness!

Nanto-Suleta: Exactly!

Then there's a long silence, in which nothing at all happens except that Sulpice smiles once. Then:

Nanto-Suleta: A snakish goldenliness plus 3.

Sulpice: Or anyway . . . three*ish*.

Nanto-Suleta: Say 2.997, 2.998 . . .

Sulpice: 2.99ak43proto-77liness . . .

Nanto-Suleta: Exactly!

They lie in silence for some 25 minutes, and then Nanto-Suleta begins to shake with quiet laughter.

Sulpice: 2.99ak43proto-77liness?

Nanto-Suleta: Yes! A citrusophical problem, I suppose!

BUT, one day . . .

But one day, Uncumber meets a man. She is trying to dial her private education channel for a session of Archaic Botany, and either she misdials or else she gets wrongly connected, because a small, wiry, bald-headed man she has never seen before appears on the screen. He looks anxious – his forehead is lined, and there are lines at the corners of his eyes. The most surprising thing about him is that his eyes are as naked as the day he was born. At the sight of Uncumber he smiles – a worried, appealing smile which somehow touches her to the heart, and makes his glasseslessness seem entirely natural.

'Tilu torku manassa manassa?' he asks gently.

Uncumber frowns, trying to protect herself against that smile.

'You're not 977-921-773-480-115, are you?' she asks heavily.

'Med nolo ga – ga skonol – ga purimi panai!' exclaims the man, still smiling.

'I was trying to get 977-921-773-480-115,' says Uncumber – thinking to herself, as rudely as she can, that the man is old enough to be her father, and for a man as old as that to go around with bare eyes . . .! But she doesn't switch off. Nor does he.

'Shepi,' he says coaxingly. 'Shepi khodkhod.' He turns his head from side to side, and then nods at her.

Uncumber realises that he wants her to do the same. She feels herself blushing at the ridiculousness of it. But awkwardly, first to the left and then to the right, she shows him her profile.

'O!' he says admiringly. 'Tavonu! Chona tavonu!'

Uncumber smiles, in spite of herself.

'Thank you,' she says.

'O, O, O!' says the man, seeing her smile. 'Guvi!' He demonstrates smiling, pushing the corners of his mouth up with his hands. 'Guvi!' he says. 'Tavonola guvi! Chona tavonola guvi!'

Uncumber can't stop smiling – it's ridiculous. She puts her two hands over her mouth to try and conceal it. This makes the man laugh. He raises his two index fingers in front of his face and inclines them both in parallel to the left. 'Kuri – u kuri falun.' He sweeps the fingers over to point to the right. 'Guvi – u guvi onsun.'

He laughs. Uncumber frowns, smiling.

'Kuri,' says the man, and he makes the gesture of wiping away tears from the corner of his eyes. 'Mor *guvi* –' and he demonstrates his smile once again. 'Mec?' he asks.

Uncumber nods. 'Yes, I understand,' she says.

The man nods, too, with a serious air. He looks at Uncumber, and spreads his hands in a gesture of helplessness – perhaps at the impossibility of communication, but perhaps, feels Uncumber, at something altogether more overpowering. He smiles his lacerating smile again. She smiles frankly back, and they look at each other, neither of them making any move to switch off.

Then the man sighs. He puts his hands to his chest

and speaks sadly, and at length. He makes a curious gesture of taking hold of the lobes of his ears and rocking his head back and forth, pulling a sad face. Uncumber nods intently, her heart melting for the man's sorrows.

'Mec?' he asks.

'Yes,' she says – and she feels she does understand, in some non-literal way – in some deeper way.

'Moru huan ao chem chem,' he says sadly, putting a hand to his throat.

'Yes,' says Uncumber.

The man sighs. Then he smiles, and makes a gesture of pushing everything to one side.

'Chom!' he says, smilingly turning his head away to dismiss what he has pushed aside. 'Chom! Chom!'

Uncumber smiles, too, touched by his courage.

'Soni,' he says gently, pointing at her as he talks, 'tavonu – kheri ao chona lisitisi ento malonuru . . .!'

She looks down and blushes at these frank compliments, which encourages him to go on. When he stops, she looks up quickly and finds that he is smiling at her.

'You've got a kind face,' she says quickly. 'I think it's a beautiful face.'

'Uh?' he says, putting his head slightly on one side and raising his eyebrows. His eyes, sees Uncumber, are brown and gentle. She indicates her own face, and then points at his.

'Handsome,' she says.

The man shrugs his shoulders cheerfully, and laughs. Uncumber laughs too. Then they both stop laughing.

A Very Private Life

'Hovi,' says the man suddenly, in a gentle, coaxing voice. 'Hovi... Hovi...'

And he beckons to her. Uncertainly she gets up from her air-couch and moves a little nearer to the reception chamber. He nods encouragingly. 'Hovi, hovi,' he says, still beckoning. She moves until she is only a few inches from where he reclines, trapped behind the transparent cylindrical wall. 'Ka – hovi, hovi!' he says, and puts his lips forward to kiss her. She hesitates a moment – then takes off her dark glasses, and puts her arms out along the wall of the chamber and her lips up against its surface. But, of course, as she and the image move forward to meet, so the image seems to dart past her and vanish; the chamber in which his image appears and the lenses which transmit hers are naturally not in exactly the same place. She finds herself with her lips pressed against inert blank plastic.

They both draw back until they can see each other again, and laugh. She slips her glasses back on.

'Cheshti,' says the man, waving his hands ruefully. 'Cheshti holovis!'

'Yes, I hate the holovision too.'

'Sansan holovis!' he says, making gestures of hitting at something. 'Modrost holovis! Puta holovis!'

'It's maddening!'

He smiles at her, and shrugs, and laughs. She smiles at him, and shrugs, and bites her lip, because she feels like crying.

'Tecu solim sinini?' he asks.

She spreads her hands helplessly.

'Sinini . . . sinini . . .' he repeats, pointing at her. 'Tecu solim sinini?'

46

But she can't understand. The man shakes his finger at her, to keep her attention while he thinks how to explain. Then he points at himself, and says slowly, 'Tecas *honim* – Noli.'

'Noli,' repeats Uncumber, gazing at him obediently, not understanding.

'Ka! Ka!' cries the man excitedly, nodding his head. 'Noli!'

'Oh, you're *called* Noli!'

'Noli! Noli! Ka! Λ – tecu solim sinini?'

He points at her questioningly.

'Oh, Uncumber.'

'Uncumber,' he repeats thoughtfully. 'Uncumber. Tavonil!'

He nods and nods, and smiles, and nods. Then he puts his hand to his forehead, as if in a military salute, and says, 'Nessom, Uncumber.'

She understands at once – he is saying good-bye!

'No – wait!' she cries in panic. 'We haven't said – I mean, how shall we see each other again?'

He puts his head on one side questioningly. She looks wildly about her for a pencil, finds none, and snatches up a stick of skin-paint instead. The only writing surface she can find to hand in her haste is herself. She writes in large, hurried figures across her chest, '977-921-773-206-302.'

'My number,' she explains. 'You will call me, won't you?'

'Ka, ka,' says Noli soothingly.

'Evenings are the best time. Oh, no, any time. It doesn't matter.'

'Choron, choron . . .'

'What's your number, Noli?' She points desperately at the figures she has written on herself, then at him. He looks about him, finds some sort of writing implement, and inscribes among the hair on his forearm, '515-214-442-305-217.'

She copies it down on her leg, among a variety of scribbled notes on Archaic Botany and other subjects.

'I mean,' she says, 'I won't call you first. I'll wait for you to call me. But I might want just to call you first – something might go wrong . . .'

They look at each other. Uncumber lifts her arms, and then drops them helplessly. He smiles at her. She starts to smile back, then looks down, her chin trembling. She tries not to cry – she's not sure what she'd be crying about, anyway – perhaps just alarm. What has she done? What has she committed herself to?

'Nin,' sighs Noli, giving his little salute again. 'Nessom, Uncumber. Shuras hov.'

'Oh! Don't go yet! There's all sorts of things I want to . . . I mean, we haven't . . . we've scarcely . . .'

'Nessom, nessom,' he says. Then with great earnestness he leans forward and points first at her and then at himself. 'Solim . . . honim . . . kala ao tisini tisini . . . Nessom.'

And he disappears.

For some time Uncumber gazes at the blank screen, and touches it – even caresses it. Then, as if nothing at all had happened, she dials Archaic Botany again, and for half an hour becomes deeply involved in the history of ragwort, milkwort, St John's wort, lords-and-ladies, and eggs-and-bacon. Then the ancient weeds are totally obliterated by a wave of anxiety. She turns them off, and copies out Noli's number over and over again on different pieces of paper, and in margins of different books, terrified that she might lose it, and with it all possible evidence of his existence.

She thinks she will never forget the last word he spoke, they were so true and perfect – when he leant forward and said 'Solim . . . honim . . . kala ao tisini tisini . . . Nessom.'

She feels that she has changed so much since the day began that she may have become unrecognisable.

Nek taomoro Noli . . .

'Oh, Cumby!' says Sulpice sadly, when she tells him about Noli (though not about his bare eyes). 'It sounds just like you, falling in love with a bald-headed man who doesn't speak the same language. You're just going to make yourself more unhappy than ever, aren't you, Cumby?'

And more unhappy than ever she does indeed become. Because the days will go by, and Noli won't call. She won't know where to put herself in her misery. She'll get up from her air-couch and walk up and down the room, she'll be so agitated – she'll wring her hands, and sigh, and wish she were at lest mildly dead. She confides in Sulpice – but can't talk to him for more than a few minutes at a time before she becomes convinced that Noli is trying to get through to her and is getting the engaged signal. So she switches off and waits on her own once again.

She calls an information channel, and hurriedly looks up the 515-214-442 area on the map. 515 turns out to be astonishingly remote, if one thinks of it in geographical terms – beyond 302, even, and bordering on the West 244 Sea. The climate is rather hot, she discovers, and there are important sea-vegetation farms along the 515-214 coast. At 515-214-442 itself there doesn't seem to be much, except seaplant processing facilities. Perhaps Noli is a decider or an envisager in the seaplant industry . . .

Eventually she surrenders pride and discretion, and calls Noli. Her hands shake when she forms the number on the keyboard, and four times she has to abandon the attempt and start all over again. There is a long wait before the number answers, during which she keeps clearing her throat, and putting her hands to her face to feel if her expression is as nonchalant as it should be, and to rearrange the set of her mouth less starkly, and settle her dark glasses more concealingly over her eyes.

At last a face appears on the screen – an indifferent-looking young man who is evidently chewing a mouthful of something. He is bare-eyed, and for a terrible moment she thinks it is Noli, and that he has changed in some horrible way – or worse, that she has entirely misremembered him.

'Isn't that . . .?' she begins. 'I wanted . . . I was trying to get . . . Sorry, wrong number.'

She switches off, and has to walk up and down her

room again, pressing her cheeks, before the turbulence caused by this unexpected deflection has settled enough for her to try forming the number once more.

Again a long wait. And again the young man's face, still chewing, still bare-eyed, still indifferent.

'Oh, God,' she says, not looking at his eyes. 'I'm trying to get 515-214-442-305-217 . . .'

Without ceasing to chew, the young man twists his head slightly and looks pained, as if he finds her incomprehensible, and culpably so.

'Isn't that 515-214-442-305-217?' she asks desperately.

'Noy?' says the young man indistinctly through his mouthful of food, looking more pained than ever.

'Please, is that 515-214-442-305 217?'

The young man shrugs and swallows.

'Por sinsin mel . . . telin fa . . .' he mutters crossly, and switches off.

Obviously it was a wrong number. But Uncumber is so cast down at getting it twice, and at hearing Noli's language used unsympathetically against her, that she cannot bring herself to try again. She feels that it was a bad augury – that two wrong numbers and the harsh use of that caressing language have flawed the magic perfection of the understanding they have enjoyed until now.

A whole day and a whole night of misery go by before she tries again. This time she orders a registered number, so that there can be no possibility of mistake.

But it is still not Noli who answers. This time it is a middle-aged woman, also with naked eyes. She has dark hair that hangs flatly down either side of her sad, anxious face, and her chest is all wrapped in cloth. She gazes passively at Uncumber, clearly expecting no good from her. She is the saddest person Uncumber has ever seen. Uncumber feels a bond with her at once – she's obviously someone like herself, who won't take Hilarin and the rest.

Uncumber shows the woman the piece of paper on which she has the number written. The woman reads it slowly, screwing up her eyes and forming each syllable with her lips.

'Kari mecu sol mimidoro . . .' she murmurs hopelessly, when she has finished.

Uncumber waves the paper about, and raises her eyebrows, in a foolish pantomime of interrogation.

'Ka, ka . . .' says the woman uncertainly, nodding.

'I've got the right number?' asks Uncumber.

'Ka, ka . . . Ka, ka . . .'

Uncumber can't think what's happening. Are there several people *sharing* a number here? How could they? That would destroy the whole point of the holovision system.

'Noli . . .' she says, trying to smile.

'Noli?' repeats the woman without interest.

'Ka, ka!' says Uncumber. 'Noli! Noli!'

She gazes about her, shading her eyes with her hand, trying to indicate that she is looking for him. The woman wearily pushes the hair back from her forehead, and sighs.

'Nek taomoro Noli,' she says.

Uncumber gazes at her, waiting for her to elucidate in some way.

'Nek taomoro Noli,' repeats the woman more loudly,

pointing out of the chamber.

'Nek taomoro . . .' says Uncumber after her, as if the words might yield up some faint savour of meaning when she tries them over on her own tongue.

'Ka, ka,' nods the woman. 'Nek taomoro Noli. Nessom.'

Uncumber presses her lips together and nods, trying to smile.

'Ka, ka,' shc says. 'Nessom.'

The physical transportation of the human body

Again and again Uncumber will try and call Noli. She gets the old woman – the young man – other men and women – even children; and all of them with bare eyes. 'Noli! Noli!' she begs them. 'Niston hona hona Noli,' they reply, shrugging their shoulders, and, 'Vos chem Noli i menu o noru,' and, repeatedly, 'Nek taomoro Noli.'

She is tortured by this repetition of 'Nek taomoro Noli.' Does it mean 'Noli isn't here just now'? Or that he's busy? Or asleep? Or does it mean that they don't know him – have never heard of him? But she feels that they do know him. They're trying to tell her *something* about him. That he's somehow gone away, perhaps?

53

People do go away – they do in certain circumstances leave their houses – that's what the emergency stairs are for. Maybe they mean he's sick? Or slightly dead?

Eventually she thinks of putting the calls through a translation centre; but if anything the results are more frustrating still.

'He is not here,' says the flat voice of the translating machine.

'Can you find him for me?'

'No.'

'Will he be back?'

'I don't know.'

'Will you ask him to call me?'

'I don't know whether this is possible.'

'Please, *please*, if you know where he is, find him for me!'

'This is none of my business.'

She believes she is beginning to go mad with the frustration of it – she catches herself clutching at her head and gasping aloud at the enormity of the situation, even uttering a little gasping laugh. She will have begun to feel by this time that her conversation with Noli was the most important event of her life – indeed, the *only* important event, the thing which gives the rest of her life meaning. It will seem to her that at some unconscious level she can recall each syllable they exchanged; that these syllables point to meanings deeper than words could express or conscious thought encompass; to ideas so seminal that they form a root system of premises from which conclusions branch out into every possible area of life – though what these conclusions are she naturally cannot articulate. And now all this is slipping away from her! Through some insane confusion she is being separated from this golden light and pushed away into a dark and meaningless periphery. The indifferent strangers on the screen have formed a line between her and Noli, to shut her out from him! When she is speaking to them she pleads with them, terrified of alienating them further. Later, she rages at them for their incomprehension and indifference – no, their comprehension and cruelty.

The idea that Noli has somehow separated himself from his holovision apparatus – has physically transported his body elsewhere – starts her thinking. It's true – the body *is* physically transportable! And if Noli can do it, so can she! In these extraordinary circumstances anything is possible. She could go *behind* the holovision network! Round the back of the world!

She begins to dream at night that she has actually taken the step, and is floating through the air, through the soft clouds of the detritosphere which glow red and gold and purple all around her, on her way to Noli. She wakes from these dreams in a state of exaltation, feeling that all her problems have been solved.

Cautiously, she asks Sulpice how people set about physically transporting their bodies.

'I mean,' she says, 'if you and Nanto-Suleta ever decide to share a house, how would you move to it?'

'That's very easy, Cumby. You just call up the service channel and ask them to send a travelling house.'

And this is what she does.

She makes certain preparations for the journey. She

takes enough solid food out of the dispenser to last her till evening; she's no idea how long physically transporting one's body about the world takes – it might take all day! She medicates herself carefully against disease, and remembering her last experience of going out through the door, she folds up a night sheet off the couch, with the idea that she can unfold it and wrap it round herself if she is afflicted by cold.

Then, without a word to anyone, she opens the secret door which she and Sulpice found so many years before, shuts it carefully behind her, and creeps up the hard, dusty stairs to wait for the travelling house.

In the travelling house

The travelling house, when it arrives, turns out to be quite comfortable and convenient. It lands on the roof right up against the door, so that when Uncumber opens the door she finds herself stepping direct from one house into the next without coming into contact with the outside world at all. Inside the travelling house there is a small room with somewhat battered upholstery and a collection of Archaic Seashells around the walls. Scarcely has Uncumber lain down on the air-couch when the holovision chamber lights up and a wrinkled, cynical face appears.

'Where to, love?' asks the face.

'515-214-442-305-217, please,' she says.

'*Where?*'

She repeats the number, made nervous by the man's incomprehension. He stares at her, in pained surprise.

'Have you any idea in your little head where 515 is?' he asks rudely.

'I think it's near 302, isn't it . . .?'

'That's right, love – near 302! Down by 348 – the other side of 196! What do you think this is – a magic carpet?'

Uncumber blushes, not knowing what to say.

'I can't take you farther than 977-921-654 – not today. You'll have to go by rocket, like everybody else. I'll take you to the rocketport. 515! God save us!'

He disappears. At once the couch comes up through the layer of air and presses into Uncumber's back, as if trying to push her up into the ceiling, and her stomach sinks down through the couch, as if it's trying to reach the floor! It's the most extraordinary and alarming sensation she has ever felt! And the whole house seems unsteady – it rolls her from side to side on the couch so that she has to brace herself against the walls. So this is what happens in the physical transportation of the body! It's not at all like the sensation of flying in her dream. No wonder it's obsolescent.

She quickly turns on the holovision, and switches it to a soothing channel. But after a moment or two the wizened face of the houseowner replaces the calm, flowing forms.

'Haven't you ever travelled before?' he asks, looking at her oddly as she hangs on to anything she can.

She shakes her head, feeling too strange to speak.
'You've got some clothes with you, have you?'
She nods.
'Well, do me a favour, love – *put them on now*, before you get out into the outside world!'

People

When she steps out of the travelling house into the rocketport a most astonishing scene greets her. People! Hundreds upon hundreds of them – all present in the flesh, together in the same enormous room!

For a moment she thinks she must be watching some gigantic holovision chamber. It's the smell which first makes her realise that she is in the presence of actual physical bodies. She recognises it; it is the delicate human smell she remembers from her childhood, when she and Sulpice climbed upon their parents and buried their faces in them – a sweet, lost, nostalgic musk, now multiplied several hundredfold so that it chokes and nauseates her.

She tries not to breathe, and pulls the sheet tightly about her to preserve herself from contagion. She is glad of the sheet. Everyone in the room is wrapped in some sort of material – often, as she sees, elaborately cut and shaped to fit the body. People stare at her, and point her out to each other. She looks for a couch to lie down on, to be less conspicuous. But there are no couches, only seats, and these all seem to be occupied already. A great many people, in fact, are sitting on boxes or bundles of possessions, or on the floor.

She is so stunned by this unexpected roomful of people that she cannot bring her mind to bear on it at all. Surely her father told her that this was what happened in the olden days, this crowding together to move from place to place? Surely it was all done away with years and years ago?

She finds a corner where she can stop to set her bearings in this extraordinary situation. The noise in the room is almost as disturbing as the stink. There are holovision chambers about the room, with soothing things happening in them, but the familiar sounds which should accompany them are drowned by all the talking that is going on, all the children's crying, all the hawking, spitting, coughing, and sneezing.

To Uncumber it seems like some old engraving of hell. And the room is so rundown and grimy! The indestructible surfaces are peeling off the walls, the rustless ceiling is rusting, the holovision chambers have been smashed loose from their mountings and bound back into place with wire. The floor is covered with abandoned packaging, dust, and in places lumps of some indescribable brown stuff which have apparently come off the shoes which people are wearing.

Some of the people nearest to her, she notices, are carrying pieces of electrical equipment, or kits of tools. And suddenly it comes to her – these people are all members of the outside classes! It's obvious, of course, as soon as she thinks about it; the outside classes *have* to travel around – they have to transport their bodies to wherever their hands are needed.

Roaming the world, wrapped in their artificial pelts – here, face to face at last, are her animals!

The ancient trackways of the air

Eventually, still feeling sick and giddy with the noise and smell of the place, Uncumber forces herself to make a move among the bodies. She finds an old-fashioned information machine – the sort of thing one sees in old tapes by Bregnil or Pin Lao-Tse – which keeps repeating 'May I help you? Ask me your questions' – in a flat, bored tone of voice. She asks it how to get to 515. 'Please wait,' grinds out the machine. 'There will be a delay of up to one minute while this information is located.' It is grotesquely archaic! It would be funny if it weren't frightening. Surely the rockets themselves aren't such hopeless relics of the past?

But they are, as she discovers when she is transported through the airlock – on a creaking mobile floor which was obsolete when Cynewulf Mbadziwe was a boy – into the rocket which is to take her on the first stage of her journey. It has seats instead of couches, and in places – not, fortunately, near Uncumber – there are holes in the walls, fitted with transparent panels!

Windows, for heaven's sake! The upholstery is torn, the floor filthy – a smell of dust and staleness mingles with the stink of the passengers.

A battered old lady clutching a case of optical instruments sits down next to Uncumber. She produces a box of garish pink pills, offers one to Uncumber, which she declines, then takes one herself and falls into a deep trance, with her head sagging irresistibly on to Uncumber's shoulder. Still, Uncumber is grateful for her presence. Only twenty or thirty seats away passengers are shouting and striking each other and vomiting on the floor; she might have been next to them.

The flight takes over an hour! And when they land Uncumber discovers that they have done only the first 4,000 miles! There is a long wait for a connection – a rocket which turns out to be even more ancient and ramshackle than the first, and which departs two hours behind schedule. By the time she reaches the rocketport at 515-214 she has been travelling for nearly seven hours, and she is too exhausted to feel anything any more. She literally staggers through the airlock into a travelling house, finds the houseowner can't understand a word she says, and only just has the presence of mind to show him Noli's number written out on a slip of paper before she collapses back on to the air-couch and weeps with fatigue, overcome by the sheet nastiness of the world she has had to traverse.

The physical transportation of the body evidently demands a mental and physical stamina which she simply doesn't possess. And the whole business of finding Noli and explaining herself when she reaches the number still lies ahead!

In the dark

When Uncumber steps out of the travelling house at 515-214-442-305-217 she steps into pitch blackness – the unlit airlock to the house, as she assumes. Standing in the little pool of light from the door-way of the travelling house, she reaches out to feel a wall to guide her. Her exploring hand sinks deeper and deeper into the darkness – the door of the travelling house shuts behind her – a cool current of air moves about her – and all at once she realises that the darkness is unwalled. She is outside, in the open! There has been some terrible mistake! She turns back to the travelling house, but already it is lifting away into the night.

She is paralysed with panic, unable to move, unable even to utter more than a wavering, inarticulate gasp of terror. The darkness and coldness of the outside night stretch indefinitely away from her in every direction! She is lost in the blackness – dissolved into nothingness by it! A violent trembling, half fear, and half cold, seizes her, and she clutches the sheet about her, standing stock still and trying not to breathe, so as not to draw the cold and the darkness and all the infections of the raw air into her lungs.

She has seen darkness before, of course. As a child

she sometimes used to cover up the dim sleeping lights at night to see what it was like. And the time she explored the emergency stairs – that was in the dark. But all this was inside, with other human beings – and the possibility of light – close at hand.

This unlimited, inextinguishable darkness of the open world is entirely different. This is the ultimate nothingness which the whole of human endeavour strives to keep at bay. How will the Kind People find her out here, in the middle of nowhere?

Gradually her naked terror subsides into something more like wretchedness. Sheer disbelief that any day could be as horrible as this one has been – and even if it could, that it could happen to *her* – overwhelms her. Misery tightens her chest; tears well out of her eyes. She hears great sobs arise and go out into the empty dark. They sound as if they belong to someone else – not hers at all.

After a while she stops crying, and takes her dark glasses off to wipe them. At once she finds that the total blackness around her is not quite as totally black as she had thought. Of course! To see in the dark you take your dark glasses off! She laughs aloud at her stupidity – a sobbing, hysterical laugh.

Not that what she can see is very reassuring. The first thing is the sky – a luminous grey overarching the blackness – and silhouetted against it the tangled branches of trees. She is in the forest! But gradually, as she becomes accustomed to the idea that seeing is after all possible, she perceives that there are no trees immediately around her. She is in a sort of clearing – the ground at her feet is flat. She bends down and stares at it through the darkness. Dimly, she makes out straight lines and angles. It is man-made – of tiles, perhaps, or bricks. They are cracked and uneven, with patches of dirt on them, and dark vegetation forcing its way through. She feels a deep sense of solace. This is not quite the primeval nothingness after all; the human race has passed this way.

As she crouches there, gazing at the surface of the ground and shivering inside her sheet, she becomes aware of a faint, regular sound in the air, which immediately seems familiar to her. Shhh, it goes, followed by a silence. Then: shhh. And again: shhh.

With great clarity the memory of those family holidays comes back to her – of certain evenings just after sunset when the wind had dropped. Of course; she is somewhere close to the sea!

She peers carefully around her into the darkness, trying to pick out some visible sign of the sea among the trees, feeling that the situation may not be impossible after all – and sees for the first time the great white figure which is standing immobile scarcely ten feet away, silently watching her!

She draws a violent, rasping breath, and feels her heart drop out of her body.

She stands stock still. So does the white figure.

A full minute goes by. Then, as the first freezing flush of terror subsides, she remembers that her eyes are exposed. She scrambles her dark glasses back on. How terrible to have stood naked before this great white beast!

For another minute she peers at the figure through the darkness of the lenses. She is shaking now as the reaction to her terror sets in. With the idea that she might be able to bring the confrontation to an end by edging imperceptibly away, she shakily moves an inch or two backwards, then waits to see if there is any reaction from the figure. There is none. She slides her feet a few more inches – and stumbles painfully on the upraised edge of a tile! She freezes, holding her breath. But there is still no reaction.

Gradually she backs away, risking a little more speed as the figure sinks back into the darkness – becomes a white blur – then just a faint patch of luminosity against the black of the forest – then nothing at all. She feels herself breathing again, as if she had not known for some time what breathing was.

But suddenly she stops. Some strange pricking at the back of her neck makes her turn round – and there, right in front of her, towering over her, is another white figure! His nose is eroded; part of his jaw is missing; his eyes are dark pits gazing sightlessly out over her head.

She screams – or hears a scream arising from where she is standing. She turns and runs – or finds herself running. The blackness rushes past her; the scream pursues her. She stumbles agonisingly upon unevennesses in the ground. Branches snatch at her face and hair; stones lacerate her soft feet. She runs until some sort of stone barrier rises in front of her at about the height of her waist and stops her progress. She lets herself fall across it and rest on it, gasping 'Oh, oh, oh, oh, oh . . .'

It's ridiculous, she sees that, because she knows now what those white figures were. They were statues – old, colourless statues made of stone, and eroded by time and weather. The stonework upon which she is leaning is a balustrade. She is in some sort of ancient *garden* – the kind of thing one sees in tapes of Shakespeare and Mwanumba – now long-abandoned and overgrown.

Gradually she stops saying 'Oh, oh, oh, oh . . .' She gets her breath and straightens up. She tries to work out some sort of plan of action, but as her panic subsides so her weariness returns. Should she try to make her way back to the point where she got out of the travelling house? She's no idea how far she has run, or in which direction it was. She would like to lie down on the ground, she is so deeply tired; but her revulsion against coming into contact with the filth and contamination of the earth penetrates even her exhaustion.

As a compromise between doing nothing and moving at random, it occurs to her to find out where the balustrade goes. She takes her dark glasses off again and begins to feel her way along it, her whole body jerking violently each time her foot presses down on something sharp. Lumps of dark, appalling vegetation force her away from it, but each time she manages to find it again. Every now and then it turns a corner, and on most of the corners an overgrown urn rises. She passes two more statues – one headless, one fallen – but feels scarcely a tremor of unease about them.

Eventually the balustrade leads her to a more open place, when the shushing of the sea is louder, and a tangy breeze stirs against her face. An orange moon is just rising through the layers of dust, casting a faint, tepid light over the tangle of vegetation and broken stone. The balustrade leads downwards, and she makes out a flight of shattered steps descending to some lower level of darkness.

Bending at each step to see where she is putting her feet, she starts down them. She is about halfway down, and is feeling with her toe for the next step, when there is a sudden double explosion – kra-*KRACK*! – of unbelievable loudness. It seems to come from the air just above her head, and it is followed by a sound like the rushing of wind.

She starts violently, and puts all her weight on the exploring foot, half catching the edge of the step and half missing it. The foot turns over with a sharp stab of pain, and she falls forwards into the darkness. Step after step catches her on the knees, breasts, and elbows as she comes tumbling down. Then the flat ground at the bottom strikes her a heavy blow across the back, knocking all the wind out of her, and she comes to rest.

She is not surprised – indeed, scarcely interested – to find that she is lying alongside two intertwined human beings. Neither of them is wearing dark glasses; two pairs of naked eyes gaze with fear and astonishment into hers.

She tries to make some remark which will sum up the situation briefly.

'Oh!' she says. 'Ohhhhhhhh . . .!'

Her two bedfellows get to their feet and hastily pull on items of clothing which are lying scattered about the ground. She herself hurriedly pulls on the dark glasses which she still has in her hand.

'Mel,' says one of her neighbours – the man – in an embarrassed voice. 'Mel modrost . . . Mel san san . . . Mel . . . Mel . . .'

To the palace

The two of them half-carry Uncumber, carefully wrapped in her sheet, through the ruined garden. She is groaning and sobbing; her ankle is incredibly painful, and she isn't used to pain. She feels in general like a doll which has been thrown violently back and forth in some children's game. 'Nonnu,' say her bearers soothingly. 'Nonnu san san tek.'

They emerge at last from the undergrowth of the garden into an open space where there are lights and the sound of human voices. On the far side of this clearing an extraordinary structure is dimly visible. It towers above them as they approach it, magnified by the uncertainty of the soiled moonlight – a massive cliff of stone, complicated with flights of stairs, great pillars, ledges, scrolls, and pediments. There are immense ornate windows – many of them roughly boarded up, with lights showing through the chinks between the boards. The word to describe the building comes to Uncumber almost at once; it is a *palace*.

On the first and broadest flight of stairs, which lead up from the ground into the heart of the cliff-face, sit a number of people, talking and laughing. At the sight of Uncumber and her bearers they shout out questions.

'Til leltomaron chomni fec tozas!' explain her bearers, disengaging arms from Uncumber and pointing back into the garden.

'Noy? Noy?' asks everyone incredulously, gathering around in excitement. One of them takes something out of a little box and makes a flame. It spurts up with a hiss, and lights up the circle of staring faces. All of them have naked eyes. More animals! Uncumber is suddenly unsure whether she still has her own dark glasses on. Her arms are caught round her rescuers' shoulders; she twitches her nose desperately and inconclusively.

'Where are my glasses?' she begs miserably.

'Noy? Noy?' asks everyone anxiously.

'My glasses! Have I got my glasses on?'

They carry her up the stairs and between the great pillars, everyone talking seriously about her, and shouting at her solicitously. More and more people gather round, lighting little flames and peering into her face. 'Til leltomaron, til huahuaron, chomni fec tozas!' everyone explains to the newcomers.

At the top of the stairs they fling open a worn wooden door, which judders against its frame. Uncumber finds herself in the light – and back inside again. But an odd inside! Odder even than the rocketport. She catches a glimpse of a worn stone floor, a staircase, and a number of door-ways. Children come running down the stairs – funny little scraggy children wearing various bits of clothing, with dirty faces and dirty feet. They come running towards the new arrivals, and stand around, silently staring at Uncumber. Women appear in the door-ways, wiping their grimy hands on their grimy skirts, and shouting after the children. When they see Uncumber and her bearers they jerk their heads up interrogatively.

'Til huahuaron chomni fec tozas!' shouts everyone,

pointing out into the garden.

'Sil . . . sil . . .' murmur the women, gazing at Uncumber and shaking their heads at the profundity of it all. 'Fec tozas? Sil . . . sil . . .'

Uncumber at last gets an arm free, and feels her glasses. They are still on her face. The gesture arouses everyone's interest, and they try to explain it to each other.

'Okon,' they agree. 'Okon chem chem.'

She puts a hand to her breasts and her knees to reassure herself that they are still intact.

'Fonfaron,' agrees everyone. 'Fonfaron chem chem . . . *Lemnon* chem chem . . .'

They carry her into one of the rooms, and lay her gently on a bed. The room is quite large, with a high ceiling that disappears into the shadows, but it is so crammed with things that its size seems inadequate. There are three beds; a large, square table; innumerable shabby chairs of every possible description; cupboards; heaps of clothing; metal cooking pots; a children's cot . . . Uncumber has never seen such a conglomeration of unattached objects in one place before.

Everyone packs into the room and crowds round the bed, gazing down at her. To avoid looking at their naked eyes she stares at the bare electric bulb hanging down from the shadows of the ceiling. Someone lifts her damaged ankle and tests it. She cries out feebly. 'Sekar,' interprets everyone, nodding wisely. They bind up the ankle and wash her cuts. Someone lifts her head and pours a little liquid into her mouth. It runs down her throat like fire, making her choke and gasp.

She sits up, pushing the glass away. It is like nothing she has ever tasted.

'Na, tavonil, tavonil!' protests everyone. 'Novos – viski! Konyak!'

She can't bring herself even to think what they might be saying. She feels like laughing hysterically – and does so. Everyone gazes at her sombrely. It's like the time she took the Hilarin. She feels she might go on laughing for ever – and at once stops, and begins to weep instead.

If this is a palace, she thinks, all these dirty, scruffy, densely-packed people – all these animals – must be kings and queens.

Her prince appears

Suddenly Uncumber realises that she knows one of the queens!

The sad woman with the hair hanging flatly down on either side of her face, who is standing at the foot of the bed gazing at her with such intent anxiety is the one she saw in her holovision chamber when she was trying to call Noli!

'I know you!' cries Uncumber, sitting up in the midst of her tears. She would like to put her arms around the woman's neck and call her Mother, she feels such a rush of recognition and affection for her. Everyone looks

71

first at Uncumber and then at the queen, who blinks uncertainly, and shifts from foot to foot. Uncumber is appalled that the woman doesn't recognise her at once.

'Don't you remember?' she says. 'We spoke to each other on the holovision.'

The queen is clearly embarrassed to be picked out and addressed with such directness. She drops her eyes, and looks sidelong at the other kings and queens.

'The holovision!' says Uncumber desperately. 'Holovis!'

Everyone understands this.

'Ah, holovis . . .!' they all repeat, nodding encouragingly to Uncumber. Some of them gesture to indicate the shape of a holovision chamber; others point to the floor, perhaps to indicate that there is a holovision chamber on the floor below. But the sad queen merely looks confused, and anxious to dissociate herself from any connection with either Uncumber or the holovision.

'Rago holovis . . .' she mutters, flapping it away with her hands. 'Orolavi holovis . . . Cheshnimini holovis . . .'

Everyone talked at once, advancing explanations to each other. One thing is plain to Uncumber already – she has found 515-214-442-305-217. This whole palace is 515-214-442-305-217! No wonder such a variety of people answered her calls! And no wonder everyone she saw on the holovision was bare-eyed – they're all outside class. She might have worked it out for herself.

She shouts over the noise! 'Noli! Noli! *Noli*!' She is determined to be heard. The word is her one point of contact with these people – her passport, as the sight of the sad queen at last informs her, to the world of kings and queens.

And it works. As soon as they hear what she is saying, all the kings and queens stop shouting and gaze at her in astonishment.

'Noli!' they repeat to each other. 'Sishti "Noli"! Skava "Noli"!'

And they all smile at her, and repeat the name, and even laugh in the pleasure of their recognition. The name is passed back through the crowd to those still jammed in the door-way and the hall outside, until she can hear them shouting the name up the stairs.

Now everyone is very cheerful. Ten people talk to her simultaneously, waving their arms and smiling. The glass is held solicitously up to her lips again, and more of the burning fluid tipped down her throat. When she chokes, half a dozen hands thump her back.

The crowd parts, and a short, bald, middle-aged man with a hairy chest, muscular shoulders, and no shirt is pushed through to the foot of the bed. He keeps looking up anxiously at the taller people all round him, blinking his soft brown eyes at them, as they explain the situation to him.

'*Noli!*' cries Uncumber, sitting up.

Noli stares at her blankly, the brown eyes blinking again, the soft pouches of dark skin around the eyes crinkling in puzzlement. For a moment Uncumber is infected by his failure to recognise her. Perhaps . . . perhaps it isn't Noli? It looked like him for a moment – but surely Noli wouldn't be so short, so old, so pouched about the eyes, so given to nervous blinking . . . ?

73

'Uncumber!' he says, in his funny Noli accent.

Uncumber's eyes brim over with grateful tears. Never in her life has anyone said anything so perfect and beautiful to her. She just sits on the bed, with a long graze across her forehead, and her ankle swollen up like a ball and the bruises coming up on her thighs and arms (all these wounds sustained in the quest for him!) and the tears running out of her eyes, liquidly watching this man of all men, this king among kings, this hairy-chested animal, lost in pleasure at his baldness, his astonishment at seeing her, his shortness, the tufts of hair in his ears, the way he rubs his hand back and forth over his mouth as he looks first at her, then sideways to right and to left at his fellow-kings, as they all shout at once, trying to tell him how they found her and brought her in.

'Skava "Holovis, holovis"!' they tell him. 'Oc skava "Noli, Noli"!'

He in his turn begins to offer explanations to them, turning from side to side to face them, spreading his hands, pushing his head forwards, referring to the holovis, and demonstrating the writing of something across his chest. Uncumber follows each gesture adoringly. All the kings in the room seem to be amused by Noli's explanation. They laugh, and slap him on the back.

'Menec Noli!' they shout. 'Menec timtim Noli!'

And they wink at Uncumber. She smiles back at them; they are all transformed by their kinship with Noli.

Only the queens seem unamused. They catch each other's eyes and compress their lips. The children gaze up into the adults' faces with open mouths, trying to follow the drama – half-smiling when they look at the smiling kings, half-frowning when they turn to the frowning queens.

Noli, feeling Uncumber's gaze upon him, spreads his hands and shrugs. Uncumber smiles trustingly back.

Now several of the queens are shouting at Noli, pointing first at Uncumber, and then upstairs. The kings humorously encourage him. Noli scratches his head, then leans first this way and then that, as if trying to lean out of something, while he puts his head on either side and talks very fast. But he is shouted down.

Uncumber keeps her eyes on him. She is confident that as soon as he has explained everything to the other kings and queens he will take her in his arms and sweep her away to some other house, where they can be alone together.

Eventually some sort of agreement is reached – though evidently not one which meets with Noli's approval. Two powerfully-built young kings lift her off the bed and force their way through the crowd with her. They take her out into the hall and up the staircase, with the whole crowd following hard upon their heels. She can hear Noli still arguing behind her as they go.

'Druv ao tork *holovis*,' he says in injured tones. 'Simni parakaminod, leptil muamuani i koro *holovis* . . . Ei! Ei! Ei!'

Poor Noli! It sounds as though they won't let him take her off on his own. They all want to look after her!

Up the broad staircase they go, then up to yet another floor, and then up a third staircase – a wooden one, this time, with steep steps, and almost too narrow for

Uncumber and her bearers. At the top of the stairs is a landing with a number of doors opening off it. Noli opens one of these doors, and they carry her into a room rather like the one downstairs, only smaller and lower, and even more crammed with things. The two young kings set her down on one of the beds.

The crowd is already swarming into the room. Noli and the two young kings struggle with them, forcing the bodies back, detaching hands from the door-posts. Uncumber feels half sickened, half excited, watching all this pressing of body upon body. The animal kingdom!

When the door is finally shut and bolted, there remain in the room not only Noli and Uncumber, but three queens, one king with a straggling black moustache, and five small princes and princesses of varying ages. To Uncumber's surprise, Noli makes no attempt to expel any of these. His family! Of course! Uncumber's heart sinks; the idea of Noli having a family never occurred to her.

The three queens go silently to a table in the corner of the room where cooking pots and earthenware vessels are stacked. Sighing heavily, the eldest of the three produces a spray of blue flames from a metal stand, and lifts a blackened pot on to them. The children all sit along the edge of a bed and stare silently at Uncumber. The king with the straggling moustache gazes gloomily at the floor, picking his teeth with his nail. Noli raises his eyebrows, sucks in breath through his teeth, and scratches the back of his head.

'Ei! Ei! Ei!' he says. 'Chen divas khodkhod . . . Chen divas khodkhod . . .!'

A colossal double explosion fills the room, like the one which caught Uncumber off balance in the garden. She jumps painfully, and puts her hands over her ears, expecting the room to burst apart in a shower of dust and smoke, as buildings do sometimes on the holovision. A dribble of white powder does come down from one corner of the ceiling, and the plates jump on the shelves.

But nothing else happens. And no one else in the room moves a muscle.

Her first night with him

Uncumber falls asleep while the others are eating. They put a plate of stuff from the cooking pot in front of her – a nightmare mess of solid brown greasy lumps and green vegetable matter, like some piece of paranoiac imagery off one of the violence channels, which she cannot even bring herself to look at. The others bend over their plates, hack at the loathsomeness with handfuls of tools, and pack it into their mouths until they can scarcely speak. The scrape of eating tool on plate, the slop-slop-slop of lips, the uneven sound of incomprehensible, half-articulated conversation, have a hypnotic effect on Uncumber in her deep exhaustion. The noises become intimate but remote; the room slips and crumples before her closing eyes.

When she wakes it is dark, and the room is full of noise of a different sort. S-n-o-o-o-o-r-e . . . *Snort*! Grunt . . .! Nkgh . . .! Kh-n-n-n-n-n-n . . .! For several panic-stricken moments she cannot think what it is, or where she can possibly be. Slowly she works it out; it is the noise of ten people sleeping, and she is in a bed. A very narrow bed – she can't move . . . something warm and solid is pressed against her, all the way down her right side. Cautiously she feels it. Another human being! Of course . . . Noli . . .! With a shock of pleasure she runs her hand over the cloth covering his broad, powerful back . . . his shoulders . . . the back of his neck (smoother, touchingly smoother, than she'd have supposed!) . . . and up into his hair (more luxuriant, voluptuously more luxuriant at the back than you'd think from his baldness!) . . . She catches her breath in her growing excitement . . . He stirs and groans . . . She feels an irresistible impulse to run her hand through the fuzzy hair on his chest . . . But there isn't any hair! It's smooth – and it bulges and folds . . . Suddenly it jerks away from her hand – struggles to sit up – turns on the light . . . is not Noli at all, but the thinnest and dourest of the queens!

Everyone wakes up. The children cry. The thin queen points at Uncumber and accuses her of – well, Uncumber can imagine what. Everyone shouts and waves his arms. Uncumber fails to explain even in her own language, and at last the light is turned out again.

After that Uncumber lies awake for hours, scarcely daring to breathe, for fear of touching the thin queen again. Her swollen ankle and her bruises have started to throb, the room is unbearably stuffy, and the noise and smell of all this sleeping humanity becomes overpowering. Sometimes she falls into a sort of delirium of overtiredness, in which she keeps moving from one weird room filled with bare-eyed people into the next, driven by the feeling that there is some correct arrangement of people and rooms, and that if only she can find it everything will come out all right. At other times she surfaces and worries about Noli. Her heart aches for him, trapped in this crowded room, surrounded by these surly queens and screaming children. How like him to share his life with all these burdensome people! To make himself responsible for all this human freight! Grunt! S-n-o-o-o-r-e! *Khnuh*! A-a-a-a-a-a-h! The whole room is heaving with life! She quite understands that he cannot express what he feels for her in these circumstances. But they will go away. She will take him away.

The cook-queen is presumably his wife; she saw when the light was on that they are sharing a bed. How like Noli to get himself caught by a woman like that! Probably when she was younger she looked plaintive and vulnerable, and he felt sorry for her. Then the large surprised queen would be her sister . . . no, *his* sister – she looks too sympathetic to be related to her . . . and the thin queen would be perhaps the wife of the moustached king, who is sleeping on the floor, or perhaps another sister . . . or sister-in-law . . .

She sinks back into the waking dream about the rooms, and is violently roused from it by another of the terrible double explosions, which makes her spring up in bed, clutching at her heart, and tangling blindly with the thin queen's limbs. This wakes the thin queen in her turn, and gives her the idea that Uncumber is assaulting her again. She fends her off, and shouts. Once more the light is turned on; once more everyone looks accusingly at Uncumber.

'I'm sorry,' she says miserably. 'I couldn't help it. It was that terrible bang . . . the *bang* . . .'

'O,' mutters the moustached king. 'Papoom.'

'O, papoom,' mutters everyone else, without interest, settling down again and turning out the light.

Uncumber spends the rest of the night rigid with apprehension; and indeed, some minutes or hours later there is another similar explosion. Then at last the strange grey light of outside day creeps into the room around the shabby curtains, and illuminates the tangle of humped bodies, limbs and open mouths. Grotesque, she thinks, and still thinking it, over and over again, falls at last into a heavy sleep.

Papoom! When she wakes again it is with another of the appalling explosions bursting in her head. But now the room is full of light, and the beds are empty. She sits up, and drags on her dark glasses.

'Noli!' she cries stupidly. 'Where's Noli?'

The only two people in the room are the cook-queen and the surprised queen. They turn round at her cry and stare at her.

'Nek taomoro Noli,' says the cook-queen.

Papoom

The surprised queen brings Uncumber a large, sawn-off fragment of some whitish substance, riddled with little air-pockets and surrounded with a hard brown skin, and when Uncumber looks puzzled, gestures to her to eat it. She breaks off a small piece and nibbles it cautiously. It's all right – more or less tasteless, in fact. She chews up several mouthfuls. It wouldn't normally occur to her to eat something that looks suspiciously like expanded polystyrene, but she finished the last of her food pills the day before, and her stomach is crying out for nourishment. The surprised queen brings her a bowl of hot brown liquid, on the top of which tiny cream-coloured specks and opalescent discs of grease are floating. She closes her eyes and sips it. It tastes remarkably like what comes out of the coffee tap.

So Noli's *nek taomoro*. That's what they said about him before, of course. She thought then it might mean he was dead! But he survived nek-taomoroing before, so perhaps he will again.

She is fascinated by the idea of the window. All she can see through it from her bed is a square of milky yellow sky. She jumps out of bed to go and take a closer look – and collapses gasping with pain on the floor, clutching her swollen ankle. It really won't bear any weight at all.

So she has to hop. But the view is worth it. The same red disc that she remembers from her childhood excursion into the outside world hangs in the same yellowy sky. The window overlooks a kind of yard surrounded by outhouses. Beyond them she can just catch a glimpse of the complex, evilly intertwined trees in the overgrown garden. They look even more alarming by day. A shock of horror goes through her to think of herself making her way among them the previous night.

But it's the yard which interests her most; there are so many things in it that she's never seen before. A number of birds are walking about, with dirty white feathers and yellow legs, pecking at the ground. A four-legged animal covered in black fur, with a tail sticking out at the back, yawns and scratches itself with one of its feet. It looks rather like a toy dog Uncumber had as a child, so perhaps a dog is what it is.

And there is a lot of machinery in the yard – rusting, broken machinery. A king appears, opens the shattered door to one of the outhouses, and drives out a travelling machine balanced on four wheels. It's all like some historical drama! Yet somehow it looks entirely natural, as if the world has always been like this.

On one side of the yard is a huge pile of what can only be rubbish – old packaging, broken chairs, rags, rotting vegetable matter. Uncumber is astonished at this. Why don't they just put it in the tube, like everyone else, and dispose of it? Presumably the tube is out of order, the way tubes get. Then why have they never bothered to have it repaired? Can't kings and queens get outsiders to come and do their jobs for them?

But, of course, these people *are* the outsiders! They *are* the animals of the world. Down in the yard – the lower animals, with feathers, or four legs. Up here – the higher animals with cloth wrapped round them, and the use of fire. This is what she always wanted to know – how the outside classes live, what the world is like outside the holovision circuits. And this is it. She gazes about her with benevolence. These are the *real* people, undistorted by holovision! This is the *real* world! She turns and smiles at the two queens in the room, trying to convey the intensity of her admiration for them and for what they represent. The surprised queen smiles a small, surprised smile back.

Papoom! Once more she jumps and trembles with shocked reaction. But she knows now what the papooms are; the whole story has come back to her. They are the noise of the ancient rockets, like the one she arrived on, passing overhead on their way in and out of the rocketport at 515 214. Once upon a time there were real kings and queens in this palace. Then the papooms came and pauperised everything in their path. Out moved the kings and queens, to take refuge in the secret burrows of the developing inside world, leaving their palaces behind as slums to house the outsiders, who have to scavenge for their homes.

But Uncumber has a romantic feeling that Noli really *is* a king; a king who refused to abandon his palace, and who proudly, sadly, hopelessly stood his ground while the barbarians swirled in around him.

A serious talk

Uncumber lies by the window all day, playing with the children when they come in, and doing her best to eat the food which the queens bring her. It becomes swelteringly close in the room as the day wears on. In a way she enjoys the discomfort. She recalls learning that the outside temperature varies from one part of the world to another – and here she is, making practical experience of the information!

When, towards evening, Noli comes in, she feels she knows so much more about his environment as a result of everything she has seen and thought during the day that he himself seems more familiar than ever. Every line of his face is as deeply ingrained in her memory as if she had known him from childhood. His hands are stained black and green, and there are more stains on his boots. A sharp, organic smell lingers about him, which she savours with pleasure.

She smiles at him, of course, and he nods and smiles at her – in a rather constrained way, as she expects, since he cannot risk revealing his real feelings in front of his wife. He pulls off his shirt and washes under the single cold-water tap in the corner. Uncumber watches every movement he makes. He sluices handfuls of water round the back of his red neck, and up over his red pate; snorts water down his nose in an irresistibly man-like way. Then he scrubs himself dry with a little worn towel, opening his eyes very wide, as if to exercise them after their immersion, his rising eyebrows pushing little red waves up his forehead to the edge of the shiny roof on top.

Meanwhile the cook-queen talks at him over her shoulder – long, rasping, impatient sentences, to which he replies with half-audible, indifferent monosyllables. Evidently exasperated, she turns and lectures him direct, pointing at Uncumber with the knife she is holding, and wagging it up and down to emphasise her points. Clearly she wants him to do something about Uncumber. He exercises his eyebrows, saying nothing. Then he puts on a clean shirt, and combs the fringe of hair round the back of his head. 'Ticini!' he says sharply to the cook-queen, and she stops her complaints at once. Then, still combing, he comes and sits down on the edge of the bed opposite Uncumber.

He smiles, and points at her ankle. She moves her head from side to side, with a wry look. He nods, and continues to comb his hair. Then he holds up his hand and raises it sharply into the air, blowing between his teeth as he does so. She watches the gesture intently, but when he puts his head on one side and raises his eyebrows she has no idea what response he wants from her. He repeats the demonstration; she shakes her head, baffled. Noli looks round at the other people in the room, rubbing his chin at the difficulty of it all. They all of them – queens, children, the king with the straggling moustache – start raising their hands on end and shooting them up into the air with little hissing blasts between their teeth. She looks mystified from one to another. Noli points at her, and goes through the performance once again. Oh, they want *her* to do it! She smiles and nods, eager to please. She raises her hand on end, shoots it into the air, and blows through her teeth. Everyone nods and smiles. They all shoot their hands into the air together. They all blow through their teeth. Uncumber is delighted to have mastered this little social usage.

But somehow they seem dissatisfied. They consult together, looking at her. Noli tries repeating the gesture, but this time, instead of blowing through his teeth, he says 'Papoom!'

At last she sees what they're driving at – it's a rocket going up! 'Papoom!' she agrees, smiling. 'Papoom!' agrees everyone, smiling too.

Then, very deliberately, Noli points at her again. At last she understands! He means, did she arrive on a rocket?

'Yes, yes!' she confirms, pointing at herself. 'I mean, *ka, ka*! Papoom! Ka, ka!'

Noli turns to the cook-queen and makes a gesture which asks, 'Satisfied?' And she seems to be – she softens, even offers Uncumber a tiny dry smile. Clearly it must have been the question of whether or not she'd arrived by rocket that they'd been arguing about earlier. Now this is settled Noli evidently wants to take Uncumber out and talk to her alone for a little. He opens the door and jerks his head for her to accompany him. She jumps up eagerly. And of course the same thing happens as before – she falls down, shouting with pain, clutching at her ankle.

At this everyone in the room grows grave again, so sympathetic are they with her suffering. The cook-queen even begins to shout at Noli and wave her knife about once more, she is so upset.

'Tisi doktor,' says Noli firmly. He picks Uncumber up bodily and carries her down the stairs. They go right back down to the ground floor – and beyond, into the basement. And there, with a dozen or so kings and children sitting around watching it, is a holovision chamber. With a word of excuse to the audience, Noli switches to a medical diagnosis channel. He holds her ankle up for the diagnostic machine to see, then listens gravely to its description of the trouble, and to its recommended cure. In one gesture he sums it up to Uncumber; his head leaning, with eyes closed, against his folded hands.

Rest. He carries her back upstairs to get some.

Just like her father said

Strange, sad days for Uncumber, sitting about the room in the damp heat, her swollen ankle stretched out in front of her. And the ankle isn't her only trouble. It's just like her father always said – the outside world is full of infections, to which she seems to have no resistance at all. For a start something goes wrong with her digestive processes. She can't bear to eat, and twenty times a day she has to go stumbling down the stairs, leaning on the stick which Noli has brought her, to the filthy lavatory on the floor below. She feels an astonishing energylessness, as if she is dying from the abdomen outwards. Then a curious prickling starts up in the roof of her mouth. It spreads downwards into her throat, somehow skinning it raw, so that she can scarcely swallow, and upwards into her head, where it swells the contents so that there is no room left to think. Tears are forced out of her eyes; streams of mucus pour out of her nose like water from a tap. Overnight, it seems to her, her personality has entirely changed. She has turned into a mindless mass of flesh; her clumsy, aching, leaking body has expanded to fill the universe, so that she is scarcely conscious of anything else. She lies slumped in the chair by the window all day like some great swollen vegetable, unable to do anything but wipe her eyes and nose on the corner of the sheet she still wears wrapped around her, and stagger downstairs to the lavatory. The children stare at her; the cook-queen shouts at her; Noli and the moustached king look at her and shake their heads.

And things get worse. An unbelievable chill comes into the sweltering air, so that she begins to shiver. She shivers more and more violently, until her teeth chatter and her shoulders shake. And yet, the air must somehow be hot as well as cold, because even as she shivers the sweat runs down off her forehead, and down her neck, and between her breasts.

The surprised queen puts her to bed, and as she lies there she becomes more and more terrified at what is happening to her. Her fingers shrink until they are nothing but ten tiny sticks. Then, as she touches them together to feel their smallness, it seems to her that they are not shrunken at all, but unnaturally large – great soft, swollen things. She hears the queens shouting at each other, and guesses they are arguing about her. But their voices seem remote and unreal, as from another world. Her sense of time becomes confused; it seems to her that she has spent a lifetime in this state. She lies gazing at the brown stains and patches on the ceiling; only they are not stains and patches – they are fat, grinning faces which come sweeping down at her, and then seem to suck her into their own tumbling, roaring, terrifying, brown-stain world.

It is dark, and she is being taken through what she is almost certain is an unreal forest by unreal people. But everything is so *muddled*! Everything changes so much as soon as you turn to look at it and see if it's unreal or not . . . !

Now it's light, and a worried face belonging to a total stranger is bending over her. The stranger is familiar, in a strange way. She believes he is called Noli . . .

Now it's dark again, and she is back in the forest . . .

At some point, either before or after the forest, one thought echoes through her brain with ironic clarity; she has escaped from the privacy of the inside world only to find on the outside a world more totally private than ever – a world entirely enclosed by the limits of her own mind.

Another trouble

And then it's light, and the sweat on her brow has dried, and she has emerged from her private world again. From blotting out the horizon all round, her body has subsided into nothingness – it seems to lie inert and helpless in the bed while her spirit darts about inside, looking out pale and clear-headed at the complexities of life in the room. Her arms are almost too weak to lift a spoon; her mouth has not the slightest desire to try talking. But her eyes follow the kings and queens, tracing the complexities of their relationships. She notes with interest to which queen each child turns to be comforted, and which child each queen picks out for blame. Three of the children belong to Noli and the cook-queen, she decides. The other two seem to belong not to the thin queen whose bed she shares, but to the surprised queen. So presumably it is the surprised queen who is married to the moustached king. It's impossible to tell from the behaviour of the kings and queens themselves. When the two kings are home they talk to each other, and the three queens seem to huddle together in a silence which is broken only when the cook-queen shouts at Noli. When the three queens are left on their own together they talk and argue incessantly. The cook-queen hectors the other two; the cook-queen and the thin queen treat Uncumber sourly, while the surprised queen joins forces with the cook-queen to brutalise the thin queen.

As Uncumber grows stronger the complex life of the room first bores and then disgusts her. Always this talk! Always these bodies cluttering the room! Always the arguments, laughter, tensions, slaps, sullen silences, yawns, belches! She remembers her room at home, with its calm and ordered life – quiet images when she wanted quiet images, people neatly encased in the holovision chamber when she wanted people. She remembers the darkness and softness of the walls, and the blessed quietness and stillness of her father and brother, maintained in perpetual chemical equilibrium. And as she thinks thoughts like these she suffers another unexpected set of symptoms. Her throat seems to swell up inside so that once again she cannot swallow. Once again the tears run out of her eyes. A sharp, sweet pain seems to strike down from her swollen throat, through her windpipe into her chest. What strange feelings! How terrible that now she has escaped into the real world all she can think about is the unreal one she escaped from! And what an ungrateful and ungracious occupant of that soft, calm, unreal world she was!

She feels that it is only the thought of Noli which keeps her from complete disintegration. Sometimes in the evening now he comes and sits on her bed for a little. He smiles, and pats her hand. He feels her brow with the palm of his roughened hand then nods and smiles. He points interrogatively at her ankle, and when she nods and smiles, he nods and smiles too.

One evening he is wearing a pair of dark glasses. She laughs at this – they look odd on him, now she has got used to seeing him with bare eyes. She tries to take them off, but he won't let her. She is touched at this unexpected concession to her world, and squeezes his hand, and runs the back of her finger through the thick scrubby eyebrows which stick out above the glasses.

'Upsid melu tem tem sesevona!' screams the cook-queen at him sarcastically, while all the children stare covertly at Noli and Uncumber from a discreet distance.

'Sish!' he says threateningly to the cook-queen without turning round. She mutters something else. '*Sish!*' he orders her. Then he smiles sadly at Uncumber.

'Temni mor,' he says. 'Sansan ferolivinil – ao kero sil for, sil ucin . . .'

She smiles. He pats her shoulder.

'Tas loro nomisti ven,' he murmurs, and sadly makes his gesture of a rocket going up into the air. 'Papoom,' he says sadly.

'Papoom,' she echoes, smiling at him confidently.

PAPOOM!! agrees a passing rocket from somewhere up in the reddening sky outside.

Out and about

Noli makes the surprised queen lend Uncumber some of her clothes, to replace the torn and filthy sheet. She feels ridiculous as she puts her arms and legs into all the special holes, and does up all the special tapes and buttons. When she first hobbles downstairs in all this rigout, feeling as weak as string after her illness, she is certain that everyone will laugh at her. But on the contrary; people evidently find her less remarkable in a dress than in a sheet. She has to sit down for a while on the marble stairs in front of the palace to get her breath. But even here, with kings and queens passing all the time, she attracts nothing more than a passing nod.

With painful slowness she makes her way on down the avenue which leads through the overgrown garden. Here and there at the edge of the road she passes statues like the ones which terrified her that first night, some fallen, and lying whitely among the dirty grass, some still standing, with broken noses, and features half worn away by time. There is a certain amount of traffic along the rutted track in the centre of the avenue – kings pushing handcarts, queens carrying bundles of clothes on their heads. Several travelling machines like the one she saw in the yard bounce by, roaring preposterously, with blue smoke coming out of pipes behind them. She sees a number of kings apparently balancing on travelling machines with only *two* wheels; what keeps them up she cannot see.

At the end of the avenue stand the eroded stone pillars of a great formal gateway. As she comes through it Uncumber finds herself face to face with the sea. She sinks down on a fallen stone to gaze at it.

It is unmistakable, of course – flat and vast and bounded by the neat horizon, just as it was on those childhood holidays. But it is not blue, as she had expected, or even green, the way she sometimes used to see it. Under the yellow sky it lies a lurid yellowish grey, shading in some places to lead, brightening in others to silver. Nor is it empty, as it used to be, but studded with complex installations built out of grey steel and rust. Between these installations machines patrol slowly up and down, roaring effortfully, with whirling wheels which sweep flashing wet vegetation out of the water into waiting hoppers. At the edge of the sea, where it moves restlessly against the beach at the foot of the bluff on which she is sitting, there is neither the sand nor the white spume which she remembers from those other seas, but a broad black scum lapping against blackened boulders.

The section of the shore where she is sitting is desolate and unused. But two or three hundred metres away to her left is a large low building constructed out of rust and disintegrating timber, and all along the coast beyond that the shore is lined with buildings, and derelict jetties, stretching out in a great arm around the bay, as if to hug the installations in the water in a huge embrace. She can see men moving through the streets. From far away round the bay there is the noise of metal striking against metal with a regular, dull, ringing sound. A whistle shrills. A deadened explosion sounds. So this is how it is, the real outside world. This is how it is.

She sits on her stone for a long time, just gazing raptly at the buildings and the water. Slowly the harvesting machines creep back and forth across their fields of sea. The black tide edges up the beach. Rockets papoom invisibly by, on their way in and out of the rocketport which must be somewhere inland behind the bay. On and on she gazes, trying to penetrate the outside world's secret, trying to seize the essential reality of it all, and soak herself in it. But the sheer uneventfulness of the scene, and the sullen warmth of the afternoon, gradually overcome her, and she dozes as she sits. When she wakes, the sea has crept under the bluff, and the copper disc of the sun swung over towards the west. But the machines are still harvesting, the remote pile-driver still hammering, and men still moving irregularly along the quays, on foot and on their two-wheeled machines. The sameness of it all begins to frighten her. Once again the picture of her own room at home comes into her head, with its dark, soft surfaces, and the sweetly varied forms which processed through the holovision chamber. Once again the familiar swelling pain comes into her throat.

Life

Each day she hobbles forth to look at the sea from one vantage point or another; and each day it is the same.

But she makes a surprising discovery. The unchanging elements of the scene are not unchanging at all if you look at them closely; the earth, the trees, the rocks, the boulders on the beach are all crawling with life. The longer and closer she looks the more shaken she is. Ants hurry in all directions through the dust, just as they do in metaphor – thousands of them, hundreds of thousands of them, disappearing into tiny holes leading down into – what? – an ant kingdom below the surface, where millions, and millions of millions of them, infest and undermine the still earth? Flies swarm over unidentifiable pieces of dark, stinking decay among the rocks. Clouds of tiny white insects of a sort she has never even heard about in all the rich treasury of metaphor hop up the beach like a dust-storm just ahead of the rising tide. Unthinkable creatures scutter through the sand at the bottom of pools. The whole world suddenly takes on the aspect of a rank heaving mass of maggots, which appears still and solid only if you stand far enough off from it. So this is what she has been protected from for all these years!

The king strikes a blow

Uncumber begins to feel that the three queens would gladly tear her to pieces if they were not so much in awe of Noli – even the surprised one would probably help, she thinks.

Their deference to him is surprising; his wife, the cook-queen, frequently shouts at him, and the other two women often seem to ignore his presence altogether. But he is undoubtedly the head of the household. When he expostulates with them in his mild way they may shout defiantly or turn their back on him – but they end up by doing as he says.

One evening Uncumber sees an extraordinary scene, which shocks and frightens her, and which perhaps explains Noli's ascendancy.

They are all sitting around the table eating their evening meal. The cook-queen is hectoring on in her usual style, casting angry glances at everyone in turn around the table, while Noli keeps his face down near his bowl, gobbling his food and saying nothing. And then, when the cook-queen pauses for breath, the surprised queen makes some mild remark. She says it so quietly, her eyes cast down indifferently, that it's difficult even to guess at the sense of it. But Noli at once puts down his eating tools and stands up. He hitches up his trousers, leans across the table, and hits her.

He hits her very hard, with his closed fist, on the side

of her face. She jerks back to absorb the blow, and her chair goes over backwards. In absolute silence everyone watches her sprawling on the floor, struggling to get her feet disentangled from the chair. Uncumber gazes at Noli, a great chill of astonishment and fear running through her. He is quietly sitting down and starting to gobble up his food again. She looks at the other two queens, to see how they have taken the incident. To her even greater surprise they are both nodding slightly, as if satisfied by the justice of it.

The surprised queen takes her place at the table again, and continues to eat, her face red, the livid mark of knuckles still visible over her left cheekbone. Uncumber pushes her food away, feeling sick. She would like to stare at Noli, to try to incorporate this new aspect of his character into her general image of him. But she daren't even glance at him. The world suddenly seems an infinitely more complex place than she ever supposed. It's not that her confidence in Noli is in any way diminished; she accepts at once that this form of behaviour is correct. It's just that she wonders fearfully what other great gaps in her knowledge of the world and of her lover's character will come to light as the days go by – what other dark corridors she will be led down with no guide but her confidence in Noli.

In fact she doesn't have long to wait for the next surprise. That night she sees the cook-queen getting into the bed which the surprised queen usually shares with the children. She looks round in astonishment for the surprised queen. She is sharing Noli's bed! And in the dark that night there are muffled gasps, and whispered words, and the rhythmic squeak-squeak-

squeaking of rusty bedsprings. So the surprised queen is not Noli's sister, but his mistress! Of course – she sees it now. She lies rigid with the covers over her head, trying not to listen. Down the long, dark corridor she goes, certain now that there are many more ahead.

Sisni

Uncumber begins to evolve a new way of thinking about Noli – perhaps a new theory of human understanding in general. The nature of his relationship with the surprised queen was completely unexpected – she freely admits that to herself. Of course, she can absorb it into her understanding of him in retrospect; she can feel with hindsight that it was unsurprising and entirely natural. A lot of one's feeling that one understands someone, she decides, consists not in the ability to know what they will do before they do it, but in the ability to accept their behaviour after the event. She doesn't know much *about* Noli – she sees that now. She thought that she knew everything about him after that first meeting on holovision. But she still doesn't know exactly where he goes during the day, or what he does. She doesn't know exactly what network of relationships and obligations surrounds him. But in some way, she feels, she knows him direct, the way she knows the feeling of sadness, or the sound of an oboe.

Some current, she feels, arcs brilliantly between the inmost him and the inmost her, jumping the unexplored tangle of circumstances between them.

One day Noli doesn't get up. He sleeps on while the queens prepare food and slap the children. Worried that he might be ill, Uncumber makes interrogative gestures in his direction, but the queens just shrug their shoulders and say, 'Sisni.'

After she has eaten, Uncumber goes and sits by his bed, partly out of anxiety for him, partly out of pleasure at having him in sight during the day. He sleeps with his mouth open; she can see the moist pink palate and the gaps among his top teeth. One arm is flung sideways, with the hand hanging over the edge of the bed, each stubby, hardened, dirt-ingrained finger curled delicately over a handful of empty air.

She studies each visible part in detail, little shocks of excitement running through her at their wornness, at the signs of their long and close contact with the world. Everything about him has been shaped by that contact. He is an artefact of reality! He stirs, and a foot emerges from the bedclothes right next to her – a worn, eroded foot, with the little toe crushed in against the rest, where the boots he usually wears press upon it. The calloused skin underneath is bright yellow, and on top there are hairs. Hairs on a foot! A rank smell rises from it. Uncumber would like to bend down and press her face against it.

About the middle of the morning Noli wakes up. The soft white eyelids roll back suddenly, and the gentle brown eyes gaze up at the ceiling, blinking sightlessly, naked and unashamed, unaware of Uncumber's gaze.

100

The tip of a leathery tongue appears and licks the dry lips. The tongue disappears, the Adam's apple moves up and down several times, and a groan labours out into the world. Then the eyelids fall shut again.

Uncumber watches the whole drama entranced, ashamed to be seeing those sweet private eyes naked in the presence of others, but excited, too, and greatly stirred by the appearance of the tongue, and the movements of the Adam's apple. Suddenly Noli seems to become aware of her presence. He opens his eyes and jerks his chin down to look at her, then hastily reaches for his new dark glasses.

He props himself up on one elbow. 'Agh,' he says, looking round and yawning. 'Agh! Hrrrrm! Khttt!' He turns his head until he can see the cook-queen. 'Chem,' he orders briefly, then stacks up the pillows behind his head, smiles at Uncumber, and pats her hand. The cook-queen brings him a bowl of food, and sullenly dumps it down next to him. He eats half of it, gobbling single-mindedly away without lifting his eyes, then puts it down on the shelf running behind the bed, and rummages about among the junk up there until he finds a little box with a luridly pretty picture on the lid of olden-day aircraft in the sunset. He takes two pills out of the box and swallows them down, smiling at Uncumber.

'Sisni,' he says. He lies down again and closes his eyes. He becomes very still. After a while his mouth falls slightly open, and a thread of saliva glistens down from one corner through the stubble on his chin. For some minutes he hums, faintly and tonelessly. A few words emerge from the depths of him, his lips scarcely moving. 'Nok . . . Lemnisil torvu ao koro . . . Sansan . . .!' His voice trails away. Uncumber sighs. Noli has clearly withdrawn into some crude version of that same private world which her father and brother used to inhabit so much of the time at home.

Sadly she goes out of the house, and makes her way down to the sea again. Her ankle is almost better, and her feet are becoming hardened to the roughness of the ground. The behaviour of the three queens suggests that as soon as she is completely better they will try to insist that she leaves. Will Noli let them throw her out? What will happen to her then? Nothing is settled – and here's another day wasted!

It is oddly still and silent everywhere, she discovers when she reaches the shore. The harvesting machines are not working. There are no noises of activity from along the coast, and the streets and quays are almost deserted. She walks along them, emboldened by the quietness. Everywhere doors are locked, windows shuttered, and machines left standing. She comes across a few queens, walking along as usual with bundles and baskets, and crowds of children running shouting through the silence. But she sees only two men, and one of those sinks wearily to his knees while he is still some way off, leans back against a wall, and slides slowly down until only his head is supported above the horizontal. So this is *sisni* – a day when men lie at home in bed, or fall down in the streets and lie on the pavement.

She goes back to the palace, exhausted by the nothingness of it all, and sits by a broken statue in the garden, watching the women gossiping on the marble stairs, and the children playing on the terraces. She goes upstairs to the room, and at the sight of Noli still lying in bed, his lips moving soundlessly, she almost feels tempted to take one of his pills herself. But how terrible, having escaped at such cost from one sort of privacy, to shut herself into another!

In the cool of the evening Noli rises, shaves, gets himself some food, and goes downstairs on to the terrace. A number of other kings are there already, Uncumber notices; and one by one, as it grows darker, all the kings in the palace come out. They sit on the steps talking, gazing out into the night, and spitting. A lot of the queens are on the terrace by this time, leaning on the balustrades above the stairs with folded arms, and talking to each other. Gradually, as if the idea has just occurred to them, the kings begin to turn round and beckon to their womenfolk to join them. Grimacing to show their reluctance, the queens leave their conversations and sit down next to their men. Packets of pills are passed round – for the women as well as the men this time, and of a different sort, whose effects are also familiar to Uncumber; for the night begins to fill with laughter. Here and there individual kings or queens attempt to tell stories, or sing songs. But their voices quaver, and trail away helplessly, defeated by the rising tide of hilarity.

Uncumber watches it all from among the children and queens still standing around the edge of the terrace. Nobody beckons to her to join the laughers on the steps – nor, as she notices, to the cook-queen or the surprised queen. For Noli is sitting with his arm round the *thin* queen, and they are gazing into each other's eyes, and laughing with the most tender intimacy.

Alone together at last

But Uncumber's turn comes.

It is in the middle of a steamy, close afternoon. She is walking along the avenue back from the sea when she hears a voice say her name quietly next to her ear – and there is Noli, astride one of the impossible two-wheeled machines, gazing at her with his bare brown eyes. She starts and blushes in astonishment at seeing him during the working day. He takes out his dark glasses and politely puts them on, then motions to her to sit in front of him on the bar of the machine. With pleasure and apprehension she does so and he turns and pedals back towards the waterfront with her balanced between his arms, her feet hanging over emptiness. The wind of their passage cools her forehead and blows her hair back into Noli's face. She clings on to his arms desperately, and laughs and laughs all the way down the avenue.

They weave slowly along the rutted dust roads of the town, Noli occasionally nodding at passersby. They stop on one of the quays, and Noli points at the sea and says a great deal about it. He gestures at the harvesting machinery, and explains it at some length. Uncumber understands entirely. 'Yes, yes,' she says, nodding eagerly; 'ka, ka.' Then they remount and ride a little farther, getting off in front of a large windowless building with a sign outside it saying 'KEL POROS pg.' It is a *siston*, Uncumber is interested to hear, where the *kara sinfil*, if she has understood aright, *temnu* every second *ao koro vas vas* with a large amount of *huahuanisi lemnos lin*. 'Ka!' she nods; 'ka, ka, ka!' They continue their tour, and Noli shows her the great factories on shore where the sea-vegetation is processed, and the immense yards where the various products are stored before being piped out to the world. They ride for miles through these yards, up long avenues between the stacks, and down interconnecting cross-streets, until Uncumber has lost all sense of direction.

Eventually they dismount. Noli carefully leans the machine up against the side of a half-demolished stack of bales, and then helps her up, climbing from bale to bale, until they find themselves in a kind of hollow on top. Uncumber gazes round, trembling with excitement. There is nothing to be seen but the fibrous black stuff in the bales, the lemon sky overhead – and Noli. She sits down on a bale and gazes up at him, shivering a little in spite of the closeness of the afternoon, knowing that where women are concerned he does not stand upon ceremony.

But with her, for some reason, he does. He literally stands in front of her, explaining something to her at ceremonious length. 'Yes, yes!' she says, through jaws clenched to stop her teeth rattling audibly together. She pats the bale next to her impatiently, and he sits down. But he doesn't even put his arm round her! He keeps talking away earnestly, even ardently. 'Kari los shemni vilivisti solim,' he says – or words to that effect. Uncumber feels that the time for talking is past. She presses up against him, and tenderly removes his dark glasses. But he hastily snatches them back, and puts them on again! Thinking that he is frightened of offending against the conventions she is used to from the inside world, she takes off her own glasses to encourage him. But this doesn't please him, either – he takes the glasses out of her hand and gently puts them back on her nose.

It's not that he's unaffectionate – he runs his hand through her hair, and rubs the backs of his fingers across her forehead, murmuring in a gentler voice things like, 'Nem divas lori sinfil oroamini,' and 'Chevon basril tenten i noro kaman . . .'

But Uncumber cuts him short. 'Hovi!' she commands, remembering what he, or his image, said in the round chamber in her own room at home. 'Hovi! Hovi!'

He leans forward and kisses her tenderly. But it's not tenderness she wants! With shaking hands she starts to undo the buttons of his shirt. 'Murm murmle!' he complains, his mouth trapped under hers. 'Murm!' she insists. 'Murmle murmle murm murmurmurm . . .!' he cries, doing the buttons up again.

She stops kissing him and gazes at him in consternation.

'Ostro asboro nec nec,' he explains, rather gruffly.

He's shy! It's because she's from the inside classes! He wants to behave with what he takes to be suitable propriety! Oh, the dear, kind, bald-headed, gentle bear! But not necessary, not necessary! She puts her arms around him, and her head on his shoulder, and squeezes him to thank him for his thoughtfulness and to reassure him that she is happy with things the way they are. But what's this? He's struggling to get his hand in the back pocket of his trousers . . . he's drawing out a little box with a romantic photograph on the lid of a man and woman kissing.

He points at it. 'Soli – honi,' he says, pointing first at her and then at himself. So it's like him and her. 'Yes?' she asks, impatient at this delay. He opens the box – it's full of pills. Great heaven, he's brought some Libidin pills for the occasion to make himself really like an insider!

'No!' cries Uncumber, shaking her head vigorously. 'Not necessary! Not necessary at all!'

And to make her point clearer, kneels in front of him, embraces his knees, and crying 'Noli! Oh, Noli!' pulls his trousers down around his ankles. Snatching unsuccessfully at his trousers he springs away from her; but, since his feet are now bound together by the trousers, falls headlong; and disappears over the edge of the stack!

'Noli!' she screams, rushing to the edge and gazing down at him. But he's all right. He's fallen into a heap of loose fibre, and is already struggling to his feet and pulling his trousers up. The only thing is, he's lost all the pills out of his box! He scrabbles wildly about among the unbaled fibre, trying to find one or two of them to take.

'What are you up to?' cries Uncumber, gazing down at him. 'Come back! Come back up here, darling.'

'Noston,' he shouts over his shoulder at her.

'Please come up, darling!'

'Noston!'

'*Please!* You can't leave me now, like this!'

'Sish! Noston tan!'

Uncumber subsides on the bales, suddenly conscious that she is shouting and panting, and that her hair is hanging down over her face. What is she doing? What is happening to her? She's not like this at all – she's romantic, melancholy, the simple trusting dog which waits patiently to be thrown a bone! And here she is behaving like a wild animal!

And so, by the time Noli has found a couple of his pills, and eaten them, and climbed back beside her, the tumult has subsided, and melancholy is undoubtedly what she is again – nervous and irritable and uncertain of herself.

'Too late, too late,' she mutters, all her old ill-temper coming to the surface once more.

'Sish!' says Noli, stroking her face, and her neck and her breasts. 'Sish!'

'Sish to you,' says Uncumber.

A close inspection of his pate

And very deft and polished he is, she has to admit, very passionate and convincing and absorbed in his work. *Too* absorbed in his work, she feels, and not enough in her. For as the Libidin takes greater and greater effect, so he seems to retreat farther and farther into himself, and become increasingly inaccessible.

She feels some pain and some pleasure. But he, she supposes, watching the sweat start forth on his polished red pate just in front of her chin, is passing through rich golden-green valleys set with towered cities, to singing uplands where the southern scent of aromatic bushes drifts in the air, and on, slowly upwards, to the towers of rose-pink rock among the mountains.

She is by no means totally insensitive to his efforts. She finds herself breathing more quickly, as she studies the interesting pattern of little veins in his naked scalp, and gasping slightly. 'Ah!' she says; 'ah! ah! ah!' meaning, 'I'm painfully conscious of the strands of dried fibre scratching my legs, and the edge of a bale pressing into my back, but all the same a most sweet warmth is beginning to spread along my veins . . .'

'Nec . . . foros liminil . . . gangan tor . . .' gasps Noli – meaning, 'Slowly I am growing light upon my feet, and slowly drifting upwards through the thin, sharp air, towards that peak where all alone I shall come face to face with the rising sun.'

For forty-seven days Noli voyages upwards, as she supposes; for three minutes she remains below. Then they settle side by side with their arms round each other, gazing up through their dark glasses into the yellowy sky.

'No-li,' murmurs Uncumber to herself slowly, trying the syllables over on her tongue.

'Cheshton arvonil . . .' murmurs Noli.

'Un-cum-ber,' she tries next. 'Do you know who the original Uncumber was? She was St Wilgefortis, the daughter of the King of Portugal, and with divine assistance she grew a beard, to protect her virginity from the King of Sicily.'

'Sansan . . .' murmurs Noli, his lips scarcely moving.

'But of course, that was a long time ago, back in the days of sailing-ships and motor-cars.'

The dancing floor

Almost every afternoon thereafter, if Noli is not at sea on the machines, where he works, they meet among the baled sea-grass. The encounters give Uncumber increasing pleasure; and as her pleasure grows, so does her despair. She was hoping that as he grows more confident of her, the need to pre-medicate his libido will disappear. But on the contrary; the more confident he becomes, the more confidently he insists on using the apparatus of the inside classes. He pills himself up with greater skill and greater discretion, but each afternoon it is not gentle, cruel, indifferent Noli who stokes her, but a de-Nolified stoker, an anthropoid stoking machine – as deft as a surgeon, certainly, as thorough as a masseur, as passionate as a politician; but also as remote and as impersonal. He soars off to his mountain-top, she to hers. She feels that she can just make him out across the valley, by shading her eyes against the light. She doubts if he can see her at all.

She has corrupted him, she realises. The world which she represents still hangs about her, even though she has rejected it. It has touched against Noli's world, and bruised it, just as wealthier worlds have always bruised and destroyed the poorer ones they have come into contact with down the ages, however good the intentions of their representatives.

She trembles with eagerness walking towards these meetings with Noli through the coppery hot afternoon. Afterwards she weeps meaninglessly, while Noli watches her with uncomprehending consternation.

Noli continues to offer her the pills, and one afternoon, in desperation, she takes two of them, hoping that in some improbable way she may find herself travelling alongside him on the road through the golden-green valley, where the blue angels trumpet over the crenellated walls of half-hidden cities. But instead she finds herself in a dark green jungle, steamy hot and full of birds whistling pure, single, flute-like notes. After many adventures she finds these birds, hovering on wings that flutter too fast to see. Whistling their single thrilling notes, the birds cluster around her, closer and closer, so that first the wind of their wings – and then the wings themselves – flutter against her arms, her legs, her face, her breasts . . .! She is a flowered creeper, next, hanging from the trees, pouring out a sweet perfume so heavy that it sinks languishingly through the air. And against her delicate scarlet petals, all up and down her, the birds' soft wings flutter . . . flutter . . .! Pollen oozes from her flowers . . . When you listen to them carefully, you realise that there is a steady rhythm in the fluttering of the birds' wings. They're like hearts which beat together. Thrrrm! Thrrrm! Thrrrm! But it's not just the birds' wings, she discovers. There are feet pounding on the beaten earth of the clearings in the jungle with the same rhythm – wildly dancing figures in strangely-figured black and white masks. Thud, thud, thud, dance the violent soft feet! They are dancing on her! They are dancing her down into the rich compost of the tropical centuries, layer by layer! She *is* the jungle floor! The masks bend low at her as they dance – and she recognises them! In stark, fearful black-and-white they express a row of yellow teeth with gaps, monstrous tufts of rusty hair sprouting from ears, a savagely corrugated forehead which goes up and up and over the top of the head, until it becomes smooth and red and shiny and marbled with tiny blue veins . . . The name of the mask is – oh, she knows it! – is Nul – oh! they are dancing on her! – is Nil – oh, oh, the whole earth is shaking! – is No, Non, None – is oh, oh, oh! the world is shaking her to pieces, and she adores it, and she is absolutely alone in the whole shaking world to enjoy it, and she hates it, she hates it . . .!

A happy time

The feeling of complete solitariness remains with her for hours afterwards, and terrifies her, driving her indoors to sit silent and shivering in a corner of the room among Noli's other women.

The idea comes to her that she is perhaps just a naturally depressive person, and that if she could cure her depression on the purely chemical level everything would be all right, or at any rate would seem so, which might in any case be the same thing. So next afternoon she takes four of Noli's happy pills before she leaves for the sea-grass yard. She starts to laugh as soon as she sees the bales. She's not sure whether it's the fact they're composed of *sea-grass* which seems so ludicrous to her, or the fact that some of the piles are *high*, and some of them are *low*. She could weep at the highness and lowness of the piles – it's the sort of thing you could break your heart over – but she decides to laugh instead.

And Noli! His baldness is a joke, a tragic joke . . . imagine someone in the inside world having no hair on his head! The hair's grown sideways, out of his ears, instead of upwards through his scalp! And the lines on his face . . .! She puts her head on his shoulder and cries with laughter, unable to look at them. What a world! What a *world*! Deft as a surgeon, passionate as a politician, he prepares the body. She lies there, sobbing with laughter. An arm lies flung on the sea-grass on her right side. Hers, no doubt! Another is scattered about on the left. Hers again! A shining red pate hovers just beyond her chin. *Not* hers! Away he stokes, this mighty stoker. And she loves it! Gasps with pleasure! Gasps with laughter at her pleasure! Gasp gasp – and what with one thing and another, scarcely a chance to draw breath! Might choke! Stop, stop! Think about something less helplessly funny. Think about Red Pate, King of the Stokers! Who *is* he, for example? There's a question! Thinking about it, she feels she may never stop laughing ever.

That

And that really seems to be that.

She goes back to the palace in a curious post-laughter mood, finds the surprised queen sitting on the steps outside, and without any forethought sits down next to her and begins to talk about Noli. She tells her everything, starting with the laughter, and how she feels everything around her is a dream, working backwards till she gets to the first time she saw him in the holovision chamber. Then she works forwards again, until she gets to her decision to leave, and retreat to the unreal world of home.

The surprised queen sympathises, particularly with

her paradoxical remarks about the unreality of the real world. 'Tana, tana, tana,' she says, shaking her head and clicking her tongue; 'ei, ei, ei!' She in turn confides in Uncumber, telling her all *she* knows about Noli. At any rate, she says a lot, pouring the words out at an unbelievable speed, and every tenth one 'Noli'; and the more she says about him, the more surprised she looks. Uncumber nods gloomily, and sighs in sympathy. Then she says *her* piece about Noli again, readjusting it all slightly in the light of her decision to leave, so that it takes on a more elegiac tone. The surprised queen does much the same. They discuss Noli up and they discuss him down, and the conclusion they reach is that he's a charlatan and a layabout and a womaniser and really just a little boy at heart – unless it was the price of food that the surprised queen was talking about all the time.

Uncumber feels greatly cheered and lightened by this heart-to-heart talk. She says good-bye to the surprised queen, and without a word to anyone else she starts off to walk to the rocketport on the other side of the bay, to get a rocket home.

On the road

It is late afternoon when she sets out. She walks through the town, and out along the dirt road which leads in the direction the rockets go as they papoom down to earth. She walks quite briskly, anxious to get to the rocketport before nightfall. But when night comes she is obviously nowhere near it – the road goes on and on into the darkness and the rockets papooming by sound just as far above her head as ever. It's unbelievable that there can be so much space between two points so close together! She's never imagined the world was built on such a scale! Even her long rocket trip out never prepared her for the size of the world as experienced by the pedestrian.

She walks on, staggering with tiredness, following the road only by its comparative lightness among the darkness of the surrounding woods, until even that fails, and she begins to wander off it and stumble over unseen obstacles at the edge. Then she feels her way into the forest, feels out a patch of ground, and stretches herself out on it to sleep. How far she has come since that first night among the trees! she reflects. To feel the bare ground with her hands! To sleep on it, with nothing but the trees and the outside air around! In spite of her aching weariness she is elated at the freedom she has won herself, and lies down happy.

But the happiness has evaporated long before dawn.

The ground soon becomes torturingly hard, and she is bitten all over by insects. The worst thing is the cold. It creeps in upon her, and she cringes into a ball to escape from it. She daren't move, for fear of letting it reach some new part of her body. But she can't keep still, because of the hardness of the ground! And when she does fall into a shallow dream (about being cold) she starts wildly awake again with the idea that she saw something move in the darkness. No doubt it was part of her dream, but the fear remains with her. She scrambles to her feet, and back to the roadway, where she runs on the spot and beats her arms about her, until the sky grows grey, and the dirt road shows clear enough through the forest for her to continue on her way without stumbling. She is hungry – so hungry that it hurts. The hollow pain gnaws away at her confidence. The feeling that she will soon be back in her own soft little room, her adventures over, recedes; it's clearly going to take her several hours to get to the rocketport. She realises that she is at her lowest point yet. From being in touch with the whole civilised world when she was at home she declined to the little circle of kings and queens in the palace, and from that she has come down again, to being entirely on her own. She feels overwhelmingly sorry for herself. As she trudges hungrily along the grey road under the lightening sky, she begins to sob.

The second day

As the day wears on she becomes very familiar with the surface of the road, since she scarcely lifts her eyes from it. It is cracked and crazed in places by the drought, and ridged by the roots of trees. There are many dry pot-holes, through which the occasional load-carrying vehicle thumps and crashes as it roars slowly by. The drivers of some of these vehicles shout remarks at Uncumber as they pass. One of them stops and opens the door of his cab, gesturing for her to climb in. But there is something about the way he grins at her which makes her frightened. She shakes her head, turns off into the trees, and waits there until he has gone.

She thinks bitterly about Noli as she trudges along. He should have realised what I felt, she thinks. He should have guessed that much. He should have had some inkling, if he'd had any real feeling for me at all. The grievance nags at her; she can't think of anything else. He should have realised, he should have guessed, he never really cared. The thought thuds through her brain, keeping step with her feet, and as the day grows hotter and she grows wearier, becomes jumbled and meaningless: he should have never really realised he should have guessed or realised, cared or realised, thought or guessed, he should have, never did, he should have. And then it straightens itself out, and pounds away at the simple heart of the proposition: he should have, should have, should have, should have . . .

Her legs ache, her bare feet are raw and tender, in spite of all her walking along the seashore, and she has to sit down. The sharp hunger pain in her stomach has gone; all she feels now is a strange dreamlike lethargy. She has the idea that she will sit there indefinitely, until someone finds her, or the world ends, or some other external event intervenes.

And when she does at last get under way again, she regrets it almost immediately, for a hundred metres farther on she finds herself faced with an impossible decision – a fork in the road, and not the slightest indication which turning to take. Her irresponsible lightheadedness persists, and giggling, she arbitrarily chooses the right-hand road; starts down it; after fifty metres changes her mind for no particular reason; and returns to take the left-hand fork.

She really has surrendered herself now into the hands of some greater power outside herself, she thinks. She feels considerable confidence in that power. It will surely provide the rocketport soon; and if it doesn't, it will provide something else – another palace or another town, with food and drink and human company. The sun passes its zenith, and burns slowly down westwards through the sulphurous sky. It is quite late in the afternoon when she hears very clearly the noise of a rocket taking off. The sound is borne on the sultry breeze and to the right of her. That greater power which set her on the left-hand road has misled her.

But it makes up for it. Peering vaguely about her, trying to decide what to do, she sees that the greater power has provided, almost exactly in front of her, a path leading into the forest in precisely the direction from which the noise of the rocket came. She starts down it with total confidence, choosing her way with what seems to her a sure instinct at every intersection. And indeed, before her confidence can finally flag, she sees the shape of buildings through the trees ahead!

When she reaches the buildings, however, they turn out to be windowless and doorless, with not a sign of human occupation. She can hear machinery throbbing, roaring, and whining inside. She finds the pipes through which the raw materials clatter and gurgle on their way into the factory; and more pipes through which the product hums smoothly out. But of drink, food, shelter, and human company – not a sign.

At this disappointment, she collapses against one of the throbbing conduits, and cries with frank despair. When she at last gets to her feet again, of course, she finds that her legs have become stiff, and that every step is intimately painful.

The path, as she now sees, stops at the factory. She returns to the last intersection, and tries a new track. But it all seems much less unambiguous now; at each new intersection she is filled with uncertainty, entirely abandoned by the greater power which had chosen for her previously. The path gets narrower and more overgrown, more obviously going nowhere. It's becoming harder to see the path at all, in fact – night is already drawing on. She thinks that she will walk until she falls, and then lie there until morning.

But the greater power has not entirely deserted her. Suddenly in the twilight she sees a complex tangle of dusty wires and pipes. It looks familiar, but at first the significance of it eludes her. She gazes at it dully, bowed by the leaden weight of her shoulders. Then with something like a flash of light inside her head, she remembers. It's exactly like the wires and pipes she saw the day she went out through the airlock, those many years ago! She must be near a house! A proper house, with proper food and proper beds, where proper people live!

With desperate energy, she follows the conduits through the trees, wading through undergrowth and flailed in the face by overhanging branches, until indeed she comes to the point where they dive down into a low, windowless building, its walls almost hidden by the vegetation of the forest. With the help of an overhanging branch, she scrambles up on to the flat roof, where the travelling houses land, to find the airlock.

The door of the airlock, however, turns out to be blind. There is no visible way of opening it from outside, and no way of drawing the occupants' attention. She hammers on it with her fists – hammers until her fists are bruised; kicks until her blistered feet can kick no more. The door remains as blind and blank as ever. If she puts her ear against it she believes she can hear the faint, distant sounds of the holovision. There are people inside, all right. But evidently they are unable to hear her. Or unwilling to.

She rests for some time against the airlock, and then hauls herself to her feet. From the edge of the roof she can just make out the line of conduits continuing into the forest. She climbs painfully down from the roof and follows them, holding on to them with both hands at every step, as if they were life itself.

It is entirely dark when she finds the next house, by stumbling painfully into the side of it. Once again she drags herself up on to the roof, and crawls about on her hands and knees feeling for the airlock. When she finds it she almost sobs with relief; there is a microphone grille next to it!

She leans towards it, not knowing what words will come out of her mouth when she speaks.

'Hallo!' she says, in a high, desperate voice which she scarcely recognises. 'I'm sorry to trouble you . . . I think I'm lost . . . Hallo? Is there anyone there . . .? Hallo . . .?'

She puts her ear to the door and listens. Not a sound. But suddenly a light comes on – a floodlight illuminating the whole area of the roof. She jumps back, shading her eyes. Glinting above the door is the lens of some sort of camera. It moves about, looking her up and down.

'Hallo!' she says to the lens, gratefully. 'I'm lost . . . I'm hungry. Can you help me, please?'

Still the lens stares at her. She panics. Perhaps it doesn't understand the language.

'Holovis,' she tries desperately. 'Hovi . . . Nek taomoro Noli . . . Papoom . . .'

She gazes at the lens pleadingly. It stops moving, and she hears a hissing sound. She just has time to wonder if this is the noise of the door opening, when a terrible stinging fire strikes into her eyes, her nose, and her throat. She staggers back, choking, and pressing her hands into her eyes to hold down that maddening pain.

They are spraying gas at her. To get rid of her. Of course! She's seen her father do it, too, when suspicious-looking outsiders came to the airlock door.

She falls off the roof in her blindness, and when the pain has begun to subside, feels her way back along the conduits to the next house. Once again it refuses to open to her. She tries a fourth house, and a fifth; and against the wall of the fifth house she finally sinks down, totally exhausted. She huddles up to it to spend the night. At least she wasn't driven away here. And she feels slightly less lonely near to other human beings, even if they are on the other side of soundproof walls, and entirely unaware of her existence.

She falls into the terrible muddled sleep of exhaustion, tormented by dreams of pipes and wires that lead on and on through the trees. Somehow, the pipes and wires are also the coldness of the night, and the hardness of the ground, and they pass through and through her.

After an hour or two she is woken by some new sensation which she can't for a moment separate out from her deathly coldness. Some cold presence is touching her with a hundred tiny fingertips all over the exposed parts of her body. It's some sort of spray! It's water spitting down over her, like a fine cold showerbath! She is soaking wet from head to foot!

It terrifies her. At first she thinks it must be coming off the house, and moves away. But still the spray comes down as hard as ever. Is it some dreadful precipitation from the trees? It's too even – too widespread. It's from the sky itself! The sky itself is leaking! It's a phenomenon she has heard about in her lessons at home – rain!

She huddles against the house wall, trying to press against the warmth and dryness of the life within. She realises, with dreadful suddenness and finality, the truth about her situation; once you've got outside the inside world, you can *never* get back in!

A moral

With unbelievable slowness the night passes, and the first grey light seeps among the trees. The forest is full of dank mist, and the endless steady murmur of the rain falling among the branches. Everywhere it comes soaking finely through the canopy of vegetation, and drips heavily off the trembling leaves.

Uncumber presses her cheek against the wet stone of the house, and strokes it, groaning. She is shivering uncontrollably; every bone in her body aches. But her lassitude is more overpowering than ever. She decides to get to her feet – but no response comes from her limbs at all. They are set rigid; and she knows that if she does manage to move them it will make her aching joints more painful still, and will disturb the cocoon of sodden clothing which has been slightly warmed by contact with her body.

When she does at last stand up it is even worse than she feared. The warm wetness round her becomes cold wetness, and her legs refuse to carry her. She collapses against the wall with a little cry, burying her face in her hands. She finds she is giggling, in a nightmarishly silly way. There is something about her doll-like weakness and the pointless accidental misery of her situation which is painfully ridiculous.

Once again she has a strong desire to surrender – to sink back to the ground at the foot of the wall, and wait in the rain for better times. Clearly she must take hold of the conduits, and follow them through the forest in the hope that they will lead to something. But it seems unbearably cruel to separate herself from the proximity of the cruel people inside the house, still asleep in their warm, dry, comfortable atmosphere, or perhaps drawing their evening meal from the tap, or watching the early-morning holovision shows.

And when she does start off, another disaster befalls her. Her dark glasses are covered with fine droplets of rain. She keeps pushing them up on to her forehead, and taking them off and wiping them uselessly on her sodden dress, but she won't give them up entirely, clinging to them as some last tenuous link with normality. And while she is going along like this, alternately blinded and concentrating on wiping, she loses the conduits! It seems impossible; one moment they're there, and the next moment they're not! She at once turns round, and tries to retrace her steps through the undergrowth exactly. But the conduits have gone.

They can only be a few metres away from her, hidden behind the dense screen of vegetation. But in which direction? With panicky despair, she casts back and forth through the trees. If she tries each direction in turn she *must* find them. But she doesn't. She tries to find her way back to the house. But all there is, whichever way she goes, is sodden green boughs which slap into her face and catch at her hair, and soaking undergrowth which engulfs her at times up to her chest.

She dare not stop to think out what she is going to do, because she knows that if she once stopped, the sheer futility of her efforts would overcome her, and never let her move again. And indeed, when at last she trips on a creeper, and falls heavily, she does not get up. She lies full length, her forehead resting on her arm, gazing at the vegetation a couple of inches in front of her eyes, which she has crushed in her fall.

It does not remain still, she notices. Little by little the wet leaves and tendrils make efforts to straighten themselves up again. She grows quite interested in the process. Millimetre by millimetre they move, in little jerks. For a long time nothing will happen, and you'd think they'd got as far as they could. Then – flick! – another minute movement. There's a moral here, she thinks, a real moral for someone in my position. And I'm going to ignore it. I'm down and I'm going to stay down. All right for the plants – they haven't been walking for two days without food or drink. I have, and I'm beaten. At last I'm beaten.

And so she lies, while the plants beneath her straighten up, and the rain above her beats down. Two dull papooms from above the clouds break the grey sky, but scarcely interrupt her train of thought, which is to do with her childhood, and Sulpice and her mother. A thin, distant whine reinforces the drumming of the rain, coming and going in the wet air like the noise of an insect. It grows louder – loud enough for her to notice it through her thoughts. It sounds familiar – something she has heard on some occasion, certainly. Then it fades again, and passes out of her mind. But back it comes, louder and louder. It seems to be coming from directly overhead. All at once she remembers; it's the sound she heard the night she was set down in the palace garden, and the day she went out of the airlock as a child – the sound of a travelling house!

Like the crushed plants, she raises herself jerk by jerk, as successive thoughts about the situation galvanise her muscles. Louder and louder grows the complaining whine. And suddenly she sees it – the outline of a house all right, black against the grey patches of sky between the trees! It is moving very slowly, just above the treetops. It is the Kind People, and they have come to save her.

On her feet at last, she waves both arms at the house. It will never see her through the trees! She opens her mouth to scream at it, but all that comes out is a strange, inadequate croaking noise. She gasps in air, and tries again.

But it's impossible, because . . . for a moment she can't even take in why it's impossible. Some terrible unseen thing is covering her mouth! And something hard and irresistible is encircling her chest, dragging her arms down against her sides! Unable to move, she feels herself being swung vertiginously backwards and downwards.

The travelling house passes on and disappears from her field of vision. Short rasping breaths are drawn next to her ear.

127

The green men

There are a dozen men sitting around in a circle on the ground under the shelter of a tarpaulin slung between four trees. They are warming their hands at a fire made of sticks, and they all gaze silently at Uncumber when her captor throws her down on the ground at their feet. She gazes up at them in terror. At first she is not even entirely certain whether they are men or beasts. Their faces are covered with shaggy hair, and from the midst of it their naked eyes gleam out wolfishly. They are dressed in filthy tatters, and ancient rusted weapons lie on the ground beside them. But they have magnificent silver rings on their fingers, and an extraordinary assortment of gadgets and ornaments on strings around their necks. They are eating – some of them proper pills, some of them the sort of heated organic mush which was served at the palace. They are eating it off richly coloured plates, and out of elegant gold and silver pill-boxes. Perhaps, thinks Uncumber, they are forest apes, tricked out in rags they have found . . . But then the ape who dragged her here speaks.

'Elle appelait les flics,' he says, nodding at her. 'Fallait la pincer, hein?'

Everyone looks at her, and then turns towards one of the group – a man who instead of sitting on the ground is reclining on a folding bed. He is eating off a jewelled plate, shovelling the food into his mouth with the blade of a jack-knife. He shrugs.

'Evidemment,' he says indistinctly, chewing.

'On ne veut pas trouver les cognes à deux pas d'ici,' argues her captor defensively. The man on the couch gazes unblinkingly and thoughtfully at Uncumber as he eats.

'Holovis . . .' says Uncumber hopefully. 'Papoom . . . Nek taomoro Noli . . .'

'Qu'est-ce qu'elle dit?' demands the man on the couch. The rest shrug.

'J' sais pas,' they say, gazing at her as they eat, like their leader.

Involuntarily, Uncumber finds herself looking not at the men but at the food on the plates, and at the canvas-covered bottles which are tipped up in the air from time to time. She feels her tongue creeping like a dried-up slug over her cracked lips.

'T'as soif, quoi?' demands the leader. He throws her his bottle, and she gulps down every last drop of water from it without stopping. It tastes of earth and metal.

'Elle sait boire, quand même,' says the leader. He turns to someone on the far side of the fire, and says, 'Eh, Dino! Donne-lui que'que chose à manger!'

A plate of the organic slush is put in front of her. No one offers her any tools to eat it with, and without waiting to make inquiries she puts her face down into it and sucks the stuff up, with her nose and chin in it. When she has finished she wipes her face on her sleeve, and shivers almost delectably.

'Une couverture pour la dame,' orders the leader, and one of the men throws her a blanket. She pulls it around her, and huddles over the fire, gazing into the flames, dissolving with contentment and gratitude. The wild men around her are frightening; but without difficulty she obliterates them from her mind, conscious only of the flames and of the warmth and fullness.

She half-dozes. Around her the conversation buzzes agreeably on, like the bees on those summer holidays of childhood.

'Qu'est-ce qu'on va faire avec la môme, ah?'

'La tuer . . .?'

'La tuer? Dieu t'envoie une fille, et tu n'peux trouver rien de plus amusant que d'la tuer . . .? On va la garder, naturellement. Pas vrai, patron . . .?'

She dozes on in the warmth. She wakes with a start when something hard hits her shoulder and the side of her head, but when she finds it is only the ground, instantly falls asleep once more. At another point she is awakened by the noise of shouting, and finds that it is coming from a face covered in red hair very close to hers. The owner of the red-haired face is trying to get under the blanket with her, and everyone else is laughing at his efforts. She gazes at him open-mouthed, too fuddled with weariness to know how to deal with the situation. But before she can do anything, the butt end of a weapon is rammed sharply into the man's chest, winding him, and rolling him over on to his back. 'Laisse-la!' growls the leader sourly, putting down his weapon, and settling back to sleep on his cot.

But even this incident vanishes from her mind almost at once, as she dissolves back into sleep again, lulled by the patter of rain on the tarpaulin.

When she awakes the next time the pattering has

ceased. For two reasons, as she slowly works out –
firstly, because the steady downpour from the sky has
stopped and given place to an irregular heavy dripping
from the trees, and secondly, because the tarpaulin has
been taken down. It's cold, too – the fire has been
stamped out. She sits up and looks around her in alarm.
The whole encampment has disappeared. The men are
standing about, their belongings in bundles at their
feet, talking and examining their weapons.

They're going! But what are they going to do about
her? Take her with them – perhaps kill her? She is
suddenly terrified. Or are they going to leave her there?
But *that* is a more frightening prospect still!

She catches the leader's bare, indifferent eye. He
motions to her to get up. One of the men takes her
blanket, folds it, and crams it into one of the packs.

The leader jerks his head. Everyone swings his load
on to his back, someone prods a weapon into
Uncumber's ribs, and they move off through the forest
in single file, with Uncumber in the middle of the line.
For a start every step she takes is almost unbearable,
her joints are so stiff, and her feet so blistered, but as
time goes on the stiffness wears off, and the blisters are
trodden numb. She is very apprehensive, too – but not
despairing, as she was the previous day; she is happier
to be in the company of her potential executioners than
on her own. And eventually her fear, like the blisters
on her feet, becomes dulled, simply by the passing of
time.

They walk for about an hour, the men moving
casually and noiselessly in spite of their burdens,
Uncumber making more noise than all the rest of the

131

party put together as she stumbles over roots and fallen branches. Once an unnoticed branch of thorns tears at her face, and she cries out, but the man in front of her turns round and hushes her with a look of such malevolence in his naked green eyes that thereafter she bites her discomfort back.

Suddenly the man in front stops; the whole line has stopped. The men squat down in absolute silence, while the leader goes on alone. Uncumber, squatting like the rest, stares down into the sodden mulch that forms the forest floor. Insects clamber over twigs, and disappear into the secret places of the earth, just as they did on the shore near the palace. The universal kingdom of the insects is still with her. She feels comforted by it now, rather than disgusted.

Something horrible is about to happen, she knows.

The leader returns, and nods briefly. Everyone gets to his feet, and begins to move slowly forward through the trees again. They have reached some sort of building. It is the house, sees Uncumber with a shock, on whose door she first beat the previous night. Or so it seems to her. With such a featureless structure it's difficult to be sure. Two of the men stand holding her while the rest pull some sort of masks over their faces and climb on to the roof. They go straight to the airlock door. But they don't waste their time knocking on it. They shine a kind of light at it, and it grows a black line from top to bottom and collapses effortlessly inwards.

Uncumber feels a curious mixture of disappointment and satisfaction at seeing the barrier on which she bruised her hands so vainly brushed aside like this. Already the men are crowding through the airlock after their leader. She knows they are going to hurt the people inside, and is appalled to find that her feelings about this are as mixed as her feelings about the breaching of the door. She bites her lip, feeling sick, waiting to hear the blows and screams.

But none comes. A minute goes by – two minutes – a long time. Then one by one the men start to emerge. They are carrying cases full of pills of every description, fabric ripped off the upholstery, jewellery, pieces of electrical equipment – even a complete holovision chamber. Uncumber recognises each item as it emerges; they are all exactly the same as the ones she remembers from her parents' house.

She is sickened at being forced to look on helplessly while this act of desecration against her own people is carried out. But she is relieved that there are after all no signs of violence, and guilty that she expected them so readily.

Last of all to emerge is the leader. He is carrying an armful of ornaments in precious metals, and a human head severed at the neck, bleeding down his trouser leg.

Uncumber's stomach leaps within her, and she clasps a hand over her mouth.

'Attention – les poulets!' shouts one of her guards at the top of his voice. Everyone stops and looks up. The familiar complaining whine is coming down from the treetops. The men throw down everything that encumbers them, and disappear like smoke into the forest. The guards throw down Uncumber; the leader throws down the head. She and it gaze at each other on the ground.

Quasil quenquenya!

The Kind People from the travelling house spread out over the scene with great speed. A number of them, wearing helmets and masks, and carrying various pieces of electrical equipment which clear a path for them through the undergrowth, go plunging into the forest after the raiders. One carefully picks up the severed head and places it inside a bag. Two more seize Uncumber.

'Oh!' she sobs. 'It was horrible . . . Horrible . . .!'

'Quasil quenquenya,' growls one of the men holding her.

'I didn't know they were going to . . . I was lost and then they found me . . .'

'Quasil quenquenya!' shouts the Kind Man, and hits Uncumber across the mouth with the back of his hand. The shock of pain and surprise silences her at once. For a moment the sheer incompatibility of the pain and the presence of her Kind rescuers prevents her making any connection between the two. When she does, a baffling dismay fills her. Surely these people are here to protect her! She would like to feel her lips and teeth, to find out what damage has been done, and where the wetness she can feel on her chin is coming from. But she can't because her hands are held behind her back.

She is taken into the house. It's frightening inside – so like Uncumber's own home, except that everything

134

has been smashed and torn. Bare wires hang out of the walls. Hot coffee runs steaming out of an open tap. The body of an old woman is crumpled up against a broken holovision chamber, her dark glasses dangling from one earpiece. Uncumber thinks of her comfortably watching the holovision only the previous evening, while she knocked inaudibly on the airlock door. So that's who it was inside – an old woman only a day away from what looks like final death. The other bodies in the house are mutilated to the point where it is impossible to imagine them alive.

The Kind People stroll about the house, yawning and whistling through their teeth, occasionally turning over a piece of wreckage with a casually inquiring foot. One of them, a paunchy man with a petulant set to his mouth, glances up at Uncumber.

'Esquamilya uquen?' he asks indifferently.

'Que usti querera unquendo,' replies the guard who hit her, shrugging his shoulders.

'I was lost in the forest,' says Uncumber quickly to the paunchy man, knowing they are talking about her. 'I was found by the men – I was captured by them – I was . . .'

'Quasil quenquenya!' says the paunchy man sharply.

'I mean,' cries Uncumber desperately, 'I'm nothing to do with them! And this Kind Man hit me . . .'

The paunchy Kind Man hits her too – another effortless, calm, professional blow across the mouth with the back of the hand. Tears of sheer pain run down her cheeks and mingle with the wetness round her mouth.

More people arrive – in white overalls and rubber

boots, this time, and carrying neat cases of instruments. They exchange jokes with the Kind Men, inspect the corpses, and shake their heads at the condition of them, compressing their lips disparagingly. The Kind People who ran into the forest return with a prisoner. It is the man who tried to get under the blanket with Uncumber – the man with the red hair all over his face. That red hair is now sticky and shining with blood which is running out of his mouth and nose, and from a gash across his scalp. He seems indifferent to his condition – as indifferent as he is to the condition of the house.

The Kind People take Uncumber and the red-headed man back with them in the travelling house. When it lands, she finds herself being led down through an airlock into a large stationary house of some sort, and put in a room by herself.

She looks round this room incredulously, unable at first to take it all in. A holovision chamber – a couch – food and drink taps – pill dispensers . . . It's a *real room*! She is back in the inside world again!

It seems impossible that she should have been restored to reality after the long nightmare outside – and restored to it by people who treated her so brutally. But here it all is again . . .! She breathes the air. It's clean and sweet – it's warm, but not too warm. She tries the taps. Real inside food runs out!

There are certain differences as compared with her room at home, it's true. The walls and floor are hard instead of upholstered – the couch is upholstered instead of air-cushioned. And there is an armoured screen between her and the holovision chamber, which makes it impossible to get at the controls and either switch it off or change the channel.

Still, all these are details which can be looked into later. She peels off the torn and filthy remnants of the clothing that Noli gave her; washes her damaged mouth and takes a pill to control the pain; showers with such luxurious pleasure that tears start from her eyes and mingle with the spray. Then she gorges herself on the food from the taps, and stretches herself on the couch.

The soothing abstract sounds and images in the holovision chamber wash over her, charming her to sleep. On the hard walls around the head of the couch she discovers there are all sorts of messages scratched – initials and dates, odd single words like 'questaya' and 'Mequiqui', and what appear to be verses. One verse, which seems curiously apt and plangent to her in her drowsy, charmed mood, reads:

> 'Querin quo requi assandi,
> Curaquod semnilo sas;
> Ornu inpactot aquandi –
> Nostraquon quamboni quas!'

She falls asleep reciting the lines over and over to herself.

At last, someone who understands

She is not free, she realises that. Freedom consists in having some control over one's transactions with the world outside oneself, and this is denied to her. She cannot reach the controls of the holovision chamber to call people up, to order goods, to seek information or guidance, to go on holiday – to determine her life in any of the ways in which free people can. All she can do is watch the abstract images provided for her – Therapeutic Sequences Numbers 3, 5, 7, 7b, 7c, 11, and D4, as the labels on them announce. She cannot even turn them off. The only way she can escape the therapy is by going to sleep, or by concentrating on the graffiti on the wall. 'Querin quo requi assandi/ Curaquod semnilo sas . . .' The lines go round and round inside her head, until they become as hypnotic as the images in the chamber.

Every now and then the images fade, and heads of one sort or another take their place. They ask Uncumber a number of questions, such as 'Quin quasilya fos endi requiquestos?' and 'Sessera quoston orna qua tengui, nil qua bonu approproquila?' In reply she can only shake her head helplessly, which satisfies some, irritates others, and eventually drives all away.

Hours or days pass; without the usual time check on the holovision there is no way of knowing. Then finally a head of a different sort appears on the screen – a sympathetic and important head, a head that speaks Uncumber's language. At any rate, every time it opens its mouth Uncumber hears her language spoken, though the movements of the mouth and the sounds which emerge seem to have no relation to each other.

'Hallo,' it says, smiling. 'Have I got this damned translating machine switched on to the right language?'

Uncumber nods, too surprised to speak. To hear her own language spoken again! She's almost forgotten what it sounds like. Even on lips which are clearly forming the syllables of some other language altogether, even emerging standard unit by standard unit from the depths of some machine, it sounds so warm and familiar and ordinary that she almost weeps.

'All right,' says the head. 'Well, my name's Omacatl. What's yours?'

'Uncumber.'

'Uncumber! That's a pretty name. Isn't that the lady who grew a beard to preserve her chastity?'

Uncumber is astonished at this – she has never met anyone before who knew.

'Oh, I know a lot of things!' says Omacatl roguishly. 'You'd be surprised! Well, Uncumber – or may I call you Cumby? – I think you and I are going to get on quite well. Don't you?'

'Well . . . yes . . . I suppose so . . .'

'I'm sure we shall. Now, Cumby, I'm a decider, among other things. Do you know what that is?'

'Oh, yes – my father's a decider.'

'Is he, indeed? Well, well. Then you know that I don't literally decide things myself – by ear, as it were.

I have a little machine to do that for me. What I have to do is to present the case to the machine: and I think I may say without boasting that the machine leans quite heavily upon my judgement. So now, to decide your case, I must obviously ask you one or two questions . . .'

But Uncumber can't understand this at all.

'What case?' she demands. 'What is there to be decided? All I want to do is to start deciding things for myself again.'

Omacatl looks rather reproachful at this.

'Cumby, Cumby!' he says, or the machine says. 'You were found breaking into a house, robbing it, and murdering its inhabitants . . .'

'No, no . . .!'

'Yes, yes! You were in the company of known Sad Men.'

'Known what?'

'Unfortunates – men with a long record of unhappy behaviour. Now what I have to decide is first, whether you yourself are unhappy in this respect; secondly, if so, how unhappy you are; and thirdly, what the best treatment would be for making you happy.'

Uncumber is so astonished and outraged that she doesn't know where to begin to explain.

'But I wasn't *helping* the Sad Men!' she cries. 'I'd been captured by them! Well, at any rate, I was lost in the forest, and they found me . . .'

'Exactly,' says Omacatl gently. 'You've got all sorts of circumstances you probably want taken into account. So you see, there's an awful lot of deciding to be done, isn't there?'

'Yes, but ...'

'Now, you say your father's a decider – a member of the inside classes. And yet somehow you were lost in the forest. Now, why don't you start right at the beginning, Cumby, and tell me exactly what happened?'

So she does. Resentfully at first, because she can't help being angry at the ridiculous assumptions which Omacatl seems to have made about her already. But he listens so sympathetically, shaking his head, clicking his tongue (or making the translating machine click *its* tongue), and murmuring 'I know, I know,' in so exactly the right places, that she finds herself warming to the task, and telling him everything – how cross-grained and obstinate she was at home; how she saw Noli on the holovision, and fell in love with him, and left home to find him; how terrible it was at the palace, and how hopeless her relations with Noli became. So engrossed does she become in the story that she starts to laugh at some of the ridiculous situations she got into with Noli, and almost to weep at other points. Omacatl smiles at her laughter, and looks cast down at her distress.

'Oh, Cumby!' he cries when she's finished. 'You *have* had some adventures, haven't you!'

She nods silently, helplessly grateful for his sympathy.

'Well, let's get all this checked. What's your mother's number?'

Uncumber stiffens at once.

'I don't think I want you to go calling up my parents,' she says. 'We didn't get on – I ran away – I want to go back on my own terms, not be brought back like, well, like a little child who's wandered into the outside world and can't get back in again.'

'Now, Cumby, be reasonable. I must let them know that you're safe and sound.'

'Well, I'm not going to give you the number, and that's that.'

Omacatl sighs.

'All right,' he agrees. 'Let's leave that for a moment, and start with your friend Noli. What's *his* number?'

'It was 515,' she starts confidently. '515 . . . 515...'

But she can't remember the rest of it. It's entirely gone out of her head!

'It was 515-something,' she says lamely.

'Everything round here is 515-something,' replies Omacatl gently. 'Haven't you got the number written down somewhere? Surely you wouldn't have set out from your parents' home without writing Noli's number down?'

Of course! She did indeed write it down, and the piece of paper is still in the pocket of the rags she was wearing in the forest!

And the rags, as she remembers as soon as she has jumped off the couch to find them, are in the waste-disposer – pulped and gone hours or days since.

'Oh, Cumby!' says Omacatl reproachfully.

'I can't help it! It's not my fault...!'

Now it's Omacatl's turn to be shocked.

'It's not a question of anybody's *fault*, Cumby. No one's suggesting it is. It's just a matter of finding out what led up to your being found on the scene of the unhappiness – whether you really were lost, or whether the whole life-story you've told me was just a fantasy from beginning to end. We have to know exactly what *sort* of unhappiness you're suffering from.

'Then we shall see if we can treat it.'

More fun with numbers

Omacatl is incredibly patient with her. It's not easy to look Noli up in the records, of course, since every one is listed under either his number, which Uncumber cannot remember, or his surname, which she never knew. Omacatl's machines do their best to work it out backwards; they find 397 Nolis in 515, none of them officially credited with a red pate, or three wives, or any of the other details Uncumber can recall. And she is forced to admit, she's not sure it isn't spelt 'Naoli', or 'Nohli', or 'Nholi'. Pressed by Omacatl, she realises that it could just possibly be 'Moli' – or 'Maoli', or 'Mohli', or 'Mholi'. Or even 'Nowli'. Or 'Mowli'. Or ...

Omacatl has a specialist examine her unconscious memory, with the aid of all the right medicaments; but though he finds a great deal of interesting lumber there whose existence she had never even suspected, Noli's number doesn't seem to have got down this far. Omacatl arranges for her to go up in a travelling house, and scan the ground beneath in the holovision chamber. But the forest looks unimaginably different from above. Noli's palace was on the coast, of course, but as she discovers, 515 is an island, with a complicated set of headlands and peninsulas, so that there is not one simple coastline to search along but several. Her muddle makes her nervous, and she positively identifies several settlements which turn out to be entirely wrong when they actually land to examine them. When at last they do find the right one the Kind People in charge of the operation have ceased to take her seriously.

'Yes, yes – this is the place!' she cries, gazing round at the dusty avenues and overgrown terraces where she was so free, and so unhappy, surprised at quite how familiar and ordinary they seem.

'Quelos quo malilya?' the Kind People ask her sceptically, looking at each other.

'I don't know – but this is the right place,' she insists.

She takes them up the familiar stone staircase and into the palace. 'Hallo!' she cries to all the various queens and children they pass. But they give no sign of recognising her! They look first at her, and then at the Kind People, and then their bare eyes go dead and remote. Not a word do they say.

Uncumber takes the Kind People up the wooden stairs to Noli's room. The sour smell that wafts out as she opens the door! If only she could make them feel the profound and melancholy echo *that* awakens in her! And there are the cook-queen and the surprised queen, hovering as ever over their cooking and washing!

'Look!' she says. 'I'm back!'

But, look as they might, they give not the slightest

144

sign of recognition. They look at her, they look at the Kind People with her, and they say nothing.

'It's me! Uncumber!' she cries. 'Just tell these Kind Men you've seen me before, that's all! They won't hurt you! I'm the one who's in trouble – not you!'

But they just stare at her, and at the Kind People, and say not a word.

'Listen,' she says desperately to the Kind People, 'I slept on that bed over there! I used to share it with the third queen – the thin one – the one who isn't here at the moment . . .!'

It's useless, of course. She turns to the queens.

'Noli!' she begs. 'Where's Noli?'

They stare at the floor.

'*Please*! Noli! *Noli*!'

'Nek taomoro Noli,' mutters the cook-queen at last.

'Quere Nolisti pereques,' translates one of the Kind People to the others. They all laugh.

' "Nek taomoro Noli",' repeats Uncumber desperately. 'I know what that means! It means Noli's at work! I'll show you where he works . . .'

But the Kind People have finally lost patience. They take her back to the travelling house. She shouts and weeps and waves her arms, but they pay no attention; they are exceedingly weary of her.

'Well, Cumby,' says Omacatl, when he sees Uncumber back in her room again. 'We've done our best. But we don't seem to have got very far, do we?'

'But we *found* the palace!' she cries. 'We found where Noli lives! Please believe me, Omacatl . . .!'

'Just Catl, Cumby.'

'Well, we did, Catl! We found it!'

145

Omacatl gazes at her thoughtfully for a long time, rubbing his finger back and forth over the bridge of his dark glasses. Then he sighs.

'I'm afraid there's nothing for it, Cumby,' he says, 'but to start right from the other end of the business. You'll just have to give me your home number, and let me check with your parents. Won't you, Cumby?'

Uncumber lies on her couch for a long time saying nothing, filled with resentment and despair. 'I suppose so,' she sighs finally.

'There's no other way to fit you back into your slot in the world. Is there, Cumby?'

'I suppose not.'

'So what's the number?'

'It's . . .'

A terrible freezing numbness seems to creep through her, obliterating the inside of her head in an icy white fog, and then creeping down to her heart.

'It's . . .'

She shivers.

'I can't remember,' she whispers.

Don't think of this as punishment

'The machine's decided your case, Cumby,' Omacatl tells her one day. 'And very reasonably, I think. It feels that there is a quite considerable degree of unhappiness involved here, and that the best chance of treating it is to re-establish you one way or another in the inside world. You're a displaced insider – I think that's as clear as anything can be. So what I'm going to do is, I'm going to chip you up to 965, and slot you into a small inside house in a development we have going up there. We're going to slot you back into the world, Cumby. Pleased?'

'But . . .'

'965-402-003-949-335, to be precise. How does that sound? Cosy?'

'But why should I be punished?' cries Uncumber. 'Why should I be forced to go and live in 965? I'm not guilty – I haven't done anything!'

Omacatl smiles sadly.

' "Guilty" – "punished"; this is a funny way to talk,' he says. 'We don't think in terms of *guilt* and *innocence*. We just ask: are you happy, or are you unhappy, so far as the evidence indicates? So don't think of this as *punishment*, Cumby – it's just the opposite. It's to make

147

you happy!

'So off you go, Cumby, and start a marvellous new life up there in 965!'

Something in the air

So off she goes, along the filthy airways, in rockets full of uncouth outsiders travelling to and from construction sites and the world's various harvests, to 965. She has no choice in the matter; when the Kind People open her door, it opens into their travelling house; when the door of the travelling house opens, it opens into the rocketport. And so on – each small section of the inside world opening inevitably into the next, through 006 to 131, and 131 to 965, and 965 to 965-402, until she arrives at last in 965-402-003-949-335.

A perfectly agreeable house it is, too. It contains only one room, but that room is scarcely distinguishable from her room at home. Soft floor, soft walls; couch, holovision chamber; all the usual supply and disposal mains. And, as Omacatl says, when, within minutes of her arrival, he appears in the holovision chamber to welcome her, she can always add more rooms when she starts a family, or marries. He will be on hand whenever she requires him, at the touch of a switch, to help her decide about taking up her studies again, to help her settle on a career, to help make all the various social and emotional relationships around which her life will be arranged.

So, constructively and optimistically, her life of rehabilitation and reintegration at 965 begins. At first her old rebelliousness asserts itself. She resents what she sees as a lack of freedom; though when Omacatl asks her in what way she lacks freedom, she can't tell him. She has full control of the holovision – can order whatever she likes to be sent – can walk out if she wants to. For some time she thinks she might try walking out. But where could she possibly go? And remembering her days in the forest, she expresses her frustration by hammering harmlessly on the upholstered walls instead. Once, in a particularly sullen rage, she manages to kick the holovision chamber to bits with her bare feet. She has to wait three days before she hears the sound of the outsiders repairing it. They are days of the most appalling nothingness, and she doesn't repeat her vandalism.

Gradually, in any case, her rebelliousness wears off. She suspects that there is something in the air which is supplied to the house, some constituent which calms and reconciles the resistant mind, and brings it into harmony with the universe. At first she is infuriated by the idea of being reconciled to the world without her consent, just as she was as a child, but before many weeks have passed she finds she has become reconciled to the prospect of reconciliation. And is reconciled even to the fact that she is reconciled to it!

So, a new Uncumber really is emerging. She accepts Omacatl's suggestion that she should take up the study of Archaic Botany again, and lets him interest her in the idea of an academic career. Reconciliation saturates her – she even becomes reconciled to the memory of Noli. He comes to seem like some lover in legend. Their incompatibility melts; her return visit to the palace with the Kind People turns into an elegiac coda to the affair. And with Noli sealed securely off in this satisfying model of the past, she finds that the way is opened to enjoy an entirely straightforward sexual arrangement with Omacatl. She lies for hours at a time, suitably medicated, beside his image on the holovision, and there's really nothing complicated or disagreeable about it at all, though she sometimes feels that the discrepancy between the movements of Catl's lips and the sounds emerging from them will always remain a very slight barrier between them.

'I suppose you make arrangements with all the women you're counselling, do you?' she asks.

'They usually find it rather helpful,' he replies. 'I don't think it would be terribly satisfactory as a permanent solution, of course. But as an interim stage, as a first step towards the network of social, emotional, and sexual relationships which we build towards in order to complete their rehabilitation, it can meet a need.'

Years go by.

Now Uncumber sees it this way. 'It was the claustrophobic atmosphere of life at home that I was rebelling against. It was the suffocating network of my family's social, emotional, and sexual relationships around me that was choking me. Now I've escaped from them into a completely new network of social, emotional, and sexual relationships, designed purely to serve my own needs, there's nothing at all to stop me being perfectly happy and well-integrated.'

'Exactly,' says Omacatl.

In any case, the world around her has not stood still all this time. Society has changed. The tightly-knit, old-fashioned world in which she was brought up – the ordered world of children and parents, uncles and aunts and grandparents, great-uncles, and great-great-aunts and great-great-great-grandparents is passing away. Nowadays people are tending to give up having children altogether and to stake their little claim upon immortality simply by living for ever instead. It was the tyranny of the parent-child and child-parent relationship which dominated society in the past, and which so intolerably violated the privacy of child and parent alike. Now that this last old, rusty lock has been forced, the shackles of blood-relationships of every sort are beginning to fall away. Of course, the new way of life brings problems of its own. When has a revolution ever been easy? But to Uncumber, as to the rest of her generation, the challenge is stimulating and absorbing.

So, her adventures over, she will live happily for ever after.

Or at any rate, until one day when something goes drastically wrong with the air-supply, and the whole house blows up, shooting her violently into the outside world once again. She falls into a deep deposit of a substance she has never seen before – snow. There are no trees in this part of the outside world; and no warmth. Just unending dazzling grey snow, stretching as far as the eye can see in every direction. Something has happened to her back in the explosion; she cannot move. She lies buried up to her neck in the pure grey softness, and the odd, dazzling light plays tricks on her eyes, causing her to have hallucinations as her consciousness fades. One of the hallucinations is her old number at home – 977-921-773-206-302 – and as it floats before her eyes it seems just as worn-looking and familiar as it did those many years ago.

She writes it out in the snow beside her before she freezes to death.

Family reunion

As soon as Uncumber is back inside a house and restored to life again, of course, she calls the number. Her mother appears in the chamber, looking calm and cheerful.

'Hallo!' says her mother amiably. 'I didn't expect to see you. They called up a day or two ago to say you were dead.'

'I was,' explains Uncumber, astonished at her mother's calmness. 'But now I'm alive again.'

Her mother switches in her father and Sulpice.

'Hallo!' they both say cheerfully in their turn. 'We thought you were dead.'

The sight of those three faces gazing so calmly out at her brings back all Uncumber's old irritation in a rush.

'You don't seem very surprised to see me,' she complains. 'I've been gone for nearly twenty years! I've been through all sorts of terrible things! I was cut off from you . . .! Alone . . .!' Her voice breaks, and she weeps – her first tears for many years. 'And all you can say is "Hallo", just like that!'

Her family gaze at her as calmly as ever.

'Cumby,' explains Sulpice, 'we thought you were dead, that's the thing. They *told* us you were dead. So of course we're all dosed up to the eyebrows with calmants and anti-depressants, to stop ourselves being distressed. That's why we can't be more surprised and pleased.'

'Well, it's disgusting!' weeps Uncumber. 'Get yourselves uncalmed! Get yourselves dis-anti-distressed, and cry, or laugh, or do *something*!'

So they take decalmants, and medicaments for heightening emotional response; and then they cry, and laugh, and all talk at once, they are so pleased to see her.

'Oh, Cumby!' they sob. 'After all these years! We thought we'd never see you again! Where have you been? Why haven't you ever called us? Oh, Cumby, your coming back like this is the most wonderful thing that ever happened! We don't know whether to laugh or cry . . .!'

And so on.

'It's just the same old Cumby!' weeps Sulpice happily. 'She hasn't changed a bit! Just as irritable and cross-grained as ever! "It's disgusting" – that's almost the first thing she said! She's lost for twenty years – and the first thing she says when she gets back is, "It's disgusting!" Oh, Cumby!'

A Very Private Life

And Uncumber takes a pill or two herself, and weeps and laughs with them to show how pleased she is to see them again.

But later on, after she has told them everything that has happened to her, and they've told *her* everything that has happened to them, and all the pills have begun to wear off, they remember how much calmer it was while she was away; and she begins to wonder just what Catl and some of her new emotional colleagues would say if they could see her carrying on like this with a lot of old-fashioned blood-relations out of the past. So they go on calling on each other for a week or two, and then, to their mutual relief, they let the acquaintance drop again.

Now Uncumber feels that she really has come to terms with the whole of her past, and settled accounts with it for good and all. Or at any rate, for the next two or three hundred years. Then a *very* strange thing happens to her. In a sudden inexplicable fit of restlessness and dissatisfaction she . . .

But that's another story.

Anthony Powell

A Dance to the Music of Time

'The most significant work of fiction produced in England since the last war.' *Clive James*

A Question of Upbringing   £2.50
A Buyer's Market   £2.95
The Acceptance World   £2.50
At Lady Molly's   £2.50
Casanova's Chinese Restaurant   £2.50
The Kindly Ones   £2.95
The Valley of Bones   £2.95
The Soldier's Art   £2.50
The Military Philosophers   £2.95
Books Do Furnish a Room   £2.95
Temporary Kings   £2.95
Hearing Secret Harmonies   £2.95

FLAMINGO

SIMONE DE BEAUVOIR

She Came to Stay £2.95
The passionately eloquent and ironic novel she wrote as an act of revenge against the woman who so nearly destroyed her life with the philosopher Sartre. 'A writer whose tears for her characters freeze as they drop.' *Sunday Times*

The Mandarins £3.95
'A magnificent satire by the author of *The Second Sex*. *The Mandarins* gives us a brilliant survey of the post-war French intellectual . . . a dazzling panorama.' *New Statesman*. 'A superb document . . . a remarkable novel.' *Sunday Times*

The Woman Destroyed £1.95
'Simone de Beauvoir shares with other women novelists the ability to write about emotion in terms of direct experience. What is almost unique, and supremely valuable, in her work is the capacity to retain a critical detachment towards her material. The women at the centre of *The Woman Destroyed* all suffer the pains of growing older and of being betrayed by husbands and children.' *Sunday Times*.

When Things of the Spirit Come First £1.95
The five women at the centre of this novel are all enmeshed in the moral and social demands of middle-class society. Even those among them who try to be rebels themselves are hobbled by their upbringing and their self-deception.
'It is because of women like Simone de Beauvoir that the prejudice and repression of which she writes no longer has such effect.' *Over 21*

FLAMINGO

Sybille Bedford

A Legacy

More than twenty-five years after its first publication *A Legacy* remains one of the masterpieces of twentieth-century literature.

'A beautiful and brilliant book.'   *Bernard Levin*

Against the background of the Kaiser's Germany and the Europe of which it forms part, two families – the Merzes, Jewish upper-bourgeoisie, and the Feldens, landed Catholic aristocracy – are joined in marriage. Out of this union emerges a political and social legacy at once magnificently funny and profound.

'One of the very best novels I have ever read.' *Nancy Mitford*

£2.50

FLAMINGO

FLAMINGO

Flamingo is a quality imprint publishing both fiction and non-fiction. Below are some recent titles.

Fiction

☐ Troubles *J. G. Farrell* £2.95
☐ Rumours of Rain *André Brink* £2.95
☐ The Murderer *Roy Heath* £1.95
☐ A Legacy *Sybille Bedford* £2.50
☐ The Old Jest *Jennifer Johnston* £1.95
☐ Dr Zhivago *Boris Pasternak* £3.50
☐ The Leopard *Giuseppe di Lampedusa* £2.50
☐ The Mandarins *Simone de Beauvoir* £3.95

Non-fiction

☐ On the Perimeter *Caroline Blackwood* £1.95
☐ A Journey in Ladakh *Andrew Harvey* £2.50
☐ The French *Theodore Zeldin* £3.95
☐ The Practice of History *Geoffrey Elton* £2.50
☐ Camera Lucida *Roland Barthes* £2.50
☐ Image Music Text *Roland Barthes* £2.95
☐ A Ragged Schooling *Robert Roberts* £2.50

You can buy Flaming paperbacks at your local bookshop or newsagent. Or you can order them from Fontana Paperbacks, Cash Sales Department, Box 29, Douglas, Isle of Man. Please send a cheque, postal or money order (not currency) worth the purchase price plus 15p per book (maximum postal charge is £3.00 for orders within the UK).

NAME (Block letters) _____

ADDRESS_____

_____

_____